Caroline Hemingway

# THE AWAKENING

## THE DESTINY CHRONICLES BOOK 1

CARROWAY

.

ISBN 978-0-9942028-0-2


Published in Australia in 2014 by Carroway

# Name Pronunciation Guide

*In order of appearance:*

| | |
|---|---|
| Imogene | IM - uh - j EEN |
| Struan | STREW- en |
| Aislinn | ASH- lin |
| Nuada | NU-ah |
| Sephtis | Sef - TIS |
| Legion | LEE - jin |
| Ryder | RI – der |
| Cillian | KILL-yan |
| Ziah | Z (long i)-uh |
| Aedan | AY- dan |
| Falstaff | FALL- stof |
| Eion | Owen |
| Rozanne | Rose- ANN |

*This book is first and foremost dedicated to:*

HAMILTON, my beloved and best friend.
Thank you for years of adventure and
inspiration.

*And second, to my children:*

MICHAELA, a Passionate Defender of Mankind
ETHAN, the Enigmatic Adventurer
ZOE, a Beautiful Dreamer
AARON, the Imaginative Explorer

You have made my life meaningful and without you
this story would never have been written. I love you all.

*This book is also dedicated to all the Foster children I
have loved and will yet love*

I am richer for knowing you and believe you will reach
your dreams.

# Prologue
## Griswold 1620

THE WIND whistled through trees with ghostly arms and creaking limbs. The moon slipped silently behind a cloud creating an eerie feeling around the little farm in Griswold. At first glance all appeared peaceful but deeper inspection revealed sinister shadows lurking in the nearby scrub. Inside the little cottage a family slept, dreaming of the day's events; oblivious to the awful tragedy about to unfold- events that would sweep them up and change their lives forever.

Mackenzie Hamilton, known affectionately as Mac by family and friends, and his wife Imogene slept soundly in the humble wooden bed crafted by his own hands. Between them lay two year old Mitchell, fast asleep and gently snoring. In the modest little room beyond slept twelve year old Struan, with his two sisters, Aislinn and Maddy. Aislinn, the elder of the two sisters, was fourteen and very responsible for her young age, while Maddy was eight and had not a care in the world. They slept soundly, snugly wrapped in the quilts their grandmother had lovingly created for them. She lived a long way away, but she loved to send her precious 'wee ones', as she called the children, as many handmade gifts as she could. These treasures were always gratefully received and the children cherished them knowing they were made with love in each stitch.

The moon peeped out cautiously from behind the clouds, bathing the intruders who silently and stealthily crept up on the little farmhouse in its silvery light. Their shadows lengthened, creating giant-like figures as they surrounded the little home, a menacing pack of wolves moving in for the kill. Their faces were obscured by animal skins and their dark clothing hid the identity of the clan they belonged to. They paused only briefly, waiting in anticipation for the moment they had come here for. At the leader's signal, they lit their torches and set the little cottage alight.

The horse neighing first woke Mac, and seconds later he became aware of the billowing clouds of smoke that clogged his nasal passages and grabbed hold of his throat in a savage grip.

'Wake up Imogene,' he spluttered, half-awake half-asleep, not quite believing their home was on fire. 'Get the children out – I think we're under attack.'

He pulled on his trousers in one motion while simultaneously grabbing his sword. The family moved efficiently and fluidly as they had practiced many times. The threat of attack was constant in the times they lived in and the children knew exactly what to do. Aislinn took hold of Mitchell and carried him tightly to her chest as he sleepily wound his little arms around her neck. Struan and Maddy held hands and ran out together into the night air, coughing from the acrid smoke that filled their lungs.

Time stood still – it felt that way to them, as though everything unfolded in slow motion. A flurry of movement, confusion as swords flashed, the moonlight reflecting off the sharp, cold steel, as the animal- like warriors attacked them. There was no mercy or compassion as the children were surrounded and herded like cattle. They clung to one another, terrified as confusion reigned. Maddy's grimy, tear-streaked face was more than Mac could bear. He roared, guttural and angry, pain erupting from him as he threw himself at these men-beasts creating a human barrier in an effort to protect his family. It was a risk he was prepared to take for the sake of them - he loved them so much and no one would take them without a fight from him. The reason for this senseless attack eluded him as his mouth formed the question.

'Why – what do you want from us?' he yelled over the chaos and the crackling fire that devoured their home. His eyes pleaded for mercy – there was none reflected. Only silence!

Hooded faces stared back at him, mysterious, their identities concealed.

'Why?' he asked again more forcefully this time.

The answer was not what he expected –a swishing, razor sharp sword that swept in a lethal arc, slicing Mac cleanly across his midriff. The children watched, horrified as he clutched his stomach, a river of red liquid seeping through his fingers onto the dusty ground; their mother viciously beaten as she pounded the back of his attacker. Mac slid to his knees, his breath raspy as he struggled to draw in oxygen.

'Papa!' The wail escaped from Aislinn's lips -pain, fear and fury spilling out. 'Stop it, you're killing them,' she begged, as she tried to shield Maddy from the horrible, bloody sight before them.

Their sweet dreams earlier in the night hour had become a nightmarish reality, their world crashing down in a matter of minutes, their loving home smouldering and spitting out hissing embers of every memory they had created. Mocking, Torturing! No mercy!

Mac lay in a bloody pool on the dusty ground, his life slipping away from him. The last the children saw of their mother as they were dragged away was her tear-streaked face as a thick rope was thrown around her neck , ready to hang her from the beautiful weeping willow that grew alongside their cottage. That beautiful tree had given the children hours of pleasure as they played and climbed it. Now it would be a constant reminder of loss and pain.

They were now prisoners in the hands of these evil men. *Who were they and why had they done this? What did they want?*

# CHAPTER 1
# CAPTURE

*Man is not imprisoned by habit. Great changes in him can be wrought by crisis - once that crisis can be recognized and understood*

— Norman Cousins

Aislinn woke feeling stiff and sore. Every muscle in her body ached and cried out in protest. Her mind was numb and she shook her head trying to comprehend what had happened in the last twenty-four hours. Painfully she recalled the horror of the night before.

'Papa, Mama.' Tears rolled from her striking blue eyes as she thought of her courageous father who fought so bravely for them. She recalled the brutality of the attack - it was all too surreal and she was still in shock.

'Get your hands off us,' she had begged as she had been dragged from her home, but the strength of men against the defenceless children had been no match and they had known it was useless to resist. She knew she had to keep herself together – that this was not the time to grieve – she had to stay strong for the others.

'You'll be sorry for what you have done to my parents,' Struan choked back his tears and spat out the threat between clenched teeth.

He was rewarded with a hard slap to his cheek, increasing his resentment.

Aislinn's heart ached worse than her body ever could - she felt as though a part of her life had been savagely ripped from her. Her beautiful face was etched with sadness and her full lips quivered just slightly. She brushed back a loose light brown curl that strayed across her face. She could not bear the thought of her parents left out in the elements for wild animals to feast on – they deserved a decent burial. She did not care how long it took her – she would return there one day and ensure they had proper graves, even if their bones were long gone.

'Don't worry Papa and Mama, I promise I'll keep them safe – I will never let them forget you.'

Nothing would keep her from seeing that happen.

Her father had often said to them, 'We're Hamilton's, we're champions, winners and favoured as a family.'

Their deep, unwavering faith in the Great One made them confident that He would never ever leave them.

She whispered weakly, but determined, 'A fine mess we're in Great One. Papa says you're always with us, and I really need you now. Please take care of our family. I don't know how to do this by myself.'

As she cried out, something filled her heart. Could it possibly be hope? It was inexplicable in the circumstances and she didn't fully understand it, but it brought her a measure of courage and comfort.

Struan stirred next to her, bringing her out of her reverie. He too was sore from the rope burns on his wrists where he had been dragged behind a horse into the dark night. His throat ached from the smoke he had inhaled and he sat up looking wild-eyed and trapped. He had dark rings around his eyes and his thick dark hair was tousled and unruly. Aislinn slipped her arm around him, comforting him in a motherly way. Usually there was rivalry between the two of them, but today he welcomed her embrace.

'Here, let me see your hands. We need to bind them – we don't want infection getting in.'

She ripped a small piece of fabric from her nightdress and gently wrapped his wrists as he winced in pain. She had always had a gentle and caring spirit about her. Her fierce sense of justice would fight anyone who exploited those who could not fight for themselves. It made her a strong person. They sat that way for a while, just watching Maddy and Mitchell sleep as though nothing out of the ordinary had happened. Neither of them spoke – words seemed pointless and each worried that a simple word would open a floodgate of emotion that would drown them all. Aislinn realized that Mitchell was not yet aware of their circumstances and would soon be waking hungry and ready for the tasty porridge that Mama usually prepared. How would she feed him? The task seemed so great and she felt insignificant and helpless. She was grateful that at least he had been spared witnessing their parent's brutal murders.

Her mind slipped back to more pleasant times. It was her way of coping with the surreal world that had descended upon them. If she could focus her mind on happier thoughts then she might just survive this ordeal. She dreamed of their family as they had been before they had left their homeland for this untamed place they called home now. Those were happy days for them. Little Mitchell was not yet part of their family then, and they had all been a lot younger. She remembered the day Papa came home and told them the news.

'We've been chosen out of all the families in our clan to go and complete some wonderful tasks for the Great One.'

His face was flushed with excitement, his eyes bright with anticipation for a future long dreamed of.

'The Elders of our clan will decide when the time is right for us to go.'

The Elders were a group of respected and wise men in the clan. Aislinn had not met any of them and was a little nervous of the power they seemed to wield; but her father assured her they were all believers in the Great One and that they spent time seeking truth and determining who would fulfill the great prophecies that had been spoken amongst the clan. It seemed their family had been chosen for the next task – prophecy never lied, nor were the Elders ever considered wrong - this was a great honour. Aislinn trusted her parents implicitly.

Initially she had felt frightened of the unknown, then a little sad at leaving the familiarity of her homeland, but that was soon replaced with excitement as she listened to Mama and Papa talking in hushed voices about the new adventure that awaited them. Their excitement and enthusiasm became contagious.

'You know we won't be able to take much with us Imogene?'

'And you know I would go to the ends of the earth with you, Mackenzie Hamilton – with or without our possessions.' She smiled at the man she had married.

'The main thing is we'll be together and doing that which was prophesied over us by the Great One.' He kissed her gently, grateful for her trusting, adventurous spirit.

Aislinn always believed they were no ordinary family. All her father's siblings had gone into the same family trade of thatching, but they were different. Papa told her stories of his encounters with the Great One many years ago as a boy. She'd sit at his feet in front of the fire and he would tell her of all the magical and wonderful experiences he'd had. She used to wish with all her heart that she would have similar experiences one day.

The prophecy foretold that Mac had been called to take people into new and promising places, to help and encourage them and to teach them about the Great One. Ever since then her father had been waiting for the right time to do these great and wonderful things.

He was an adventurous man who loved new challenges and lived his life with passion and enthusiasm that left others envious of him. The thing Aislinn loved most about her father was his optimism. He was the most positive person and this coupled with his infectious laugh made him extremely likeable.

Not all the family shared the same enthusiasm when it came to Mac taking his family off into the unknown. Of course his brothers had scratched their heads in wonder and teased him mercilessly.

'Why do you want to go off on what could be an extremely perilous journey with your children and Imogene? Have you thought how this could affect them? We think it is irresponsible Mac.'

The harder they tried to dissuade him the more their scepticism and ridicule made him more determined than ever to follow his dream and not the path set out for him by the family trade. Mac's mind was made up –their course mapped out. The Prophecy had to be fulfilled.

So after many years of faithfully serving, Papa was appointed as an Elder of the clan. He became well respected amongst our people and served them well.

Any dream can become a reality if you believe in it and hold fast to it. Aislinn remembered the day things changed after her parents met with the other Elders, but they divulged no information to the children but she could tell by their hushed tones that something was afoot.

'What's happening?' Struan asked, curiosity getting the better of him. 'Do we know yet where we are going and when we will be leaving?'

'No, I don't know – I've been trying to listen to Mama and Papa's conversation but they're not letting anything slip yet' Aislinn let out a sigh.

'Well I hope we aren't leaving just yet. We have a school dance in the village next week and Duncan says that Becky wants to go with me.'

'Ah yes, beautiful Becky,' teased Aislinn as her brother tried hitting her with a piece of his bread crust as he flung it across the room. He could not hide the deep flush on his cheeks.

Over the following weeks the children discovered their plans. Their parents could no longer keep the excitement they felt hidden from the children. Their enthusiasm was contagious and the children themselves found the idea of new adventure exhilarating. That is the joy of being a child – the luxury to feel secure and safe no matter what you face because of trust and love. They would be leaving their homeland and traveling to Griswold, a hostile and difficult land full of mystical and untamed creatures and people.

'It'll be a challenge for us but the Great One will be with us and he'll protect us as we go,' her father reassured them. They believed him of course.

To Aislinn and her siblings, the Great One was often spoken of by Papa and Mama – they had faith in him because their parents had talked of his love, but in truth they had never really experienced the Great One for themselves.

Maddy, as always, was curious about the move and asked a million questions.

'How will we know which village in Griswold to stay in?'

'Don't you worry about that Maddy. The Great One will direct our journey and show us a sign when we get there.' Mac kissed the top of her head and was rewarded with an adoring smile from his trusting daughter.

The horror stories of Griswold had not escaped Aislinn's ears over the years. She'd heard there were warriors who worked for someone called The Dark Lord who lived for destruction and bloodshed. Tales of creatures of incredible size and ferocity were abundant - dragons in Griswold that would crush you with one blow of their tails or fiery flames from their nostrils that would turn you to ash. There was another legend that if the Dark Lord looked upon you, that you'd become bewitched and that your heart would turn black never to be redeemed again - that was an even more terrifying thought than meeting a dragon.

Mackenzie and Imogene Hamilton were wise in teaching their children about the goodness of the Great One they followed, but they had also revealed some stories to their children about the Dark Lord. He was one who wanted to rule and reign over as many kingdoms as he could. Griswold was just the tip of his iceberg dream. He was ambitious and would stop at nothing to get his own way - he would stand on anyone who hindered his progress. He never played fair or by the rules.

'Be very careful of him as he will try to steal your heart with flattering words and promises of the world, but that is to cloud your judgment and confuse your mind. Nothing he tells you can ever be believed or trusted.'

It was well known the Dark Lord was the complete opposite of the Great One. The two had been at loggerheads for many years and the Dark Lord's greatest desire and wish was to be more powerful than the Great One. He would do anything to achieve that purpose. While the Great One was generous, kind and loving; the Dark Lord was evil, cruel and full of hatred.

Aislinn stirred from her reverie, bringing her sharply back to the reality of their situation. She heard raised voices outside their tent. Two men were having an angry confrontation and seemed to be arguing over the events of the night before. She strained to hear what they were saying.

'You promised no one would be hurt and that we were just there to scare the family,' the first voice said.

'The Dark Lord's not interested in scaring people,' the other man snorted. 'He wants to eradicate those who are troublesome to him, especially those called by the Great One, like Mackenzie Hamilton and his family. The only reason we kept the children alive is because he believes they can be used to serve his purposes.'

'I don't like being manipulated and lied to. If he expects us to do his dirty work, then he should at least be honest about his intentions,' the first man grumbled. It was clear he was agitated. This deception had caught him off-guard, and now he was equally responsible for the destruction that had been caused.

'Don't be so naïve. For what is truth really? Truth can be manipulated depending on the way it is presented as the Hamilton family will find out. You were as much a part in believing what was said about them as any of us, so man up and take responsibility. Get ready we are heading out shortly – your reward will come when we deliver these children.'

Aislinn fell back against the soft fur pelt she was lying on. It dawned on her that the reason for the attack was not random, but because they were seen as a threat to the Dark Lord and his kingdom. This baffled her. She thought of her father's contagious laughter and charismatic personality, how he loved life and all the challenges that came their way. Why would anyone be intimidated by them? They only ever wanted the best for the people in their village and they tried to encourage people to believe that they could reach for the stars if they so wished. Surely that was a good and noble thing? Surely that would ultimately benefit Griswold? What did that man mean by his last comment? What did they believe about their family? None of it made any sense to her. Were they really so influential? One thing she knew for sure – they were on their way to the Dark Lord and the thought terrified her.

The tent flap drew open with a slapping sound and a cloaked man peered inside. Aislinn recoiled, struggling with terror and fierce maternal instinct to protect her brothers and sister. She recognized him as the man who killed her father and mother. Instinctively she placed herself between her siblings and this heartless man. He looked at her coldly, with lifeless, empty eyes devoid of any compassion or pity. His face was in shadow but there was no mistaking the cruelty there or his menacing posture as he filled the tent entrance.

Something about him really bothered her – he seemed familiar but she could not quite work out what it was. Her mind urged her to remember but she could not. He heart felt that she knew him, but her mind and eyes told a different story.

'Wake your family,' he barked, 'We need to be going soon, as the Dark Lord awaits us.'

She plucked up as much courage as she could.

'Please could we have something to eat?'

For an instant she detected a glint of respect in his eyes, but it was gone as quickly as she perceived it.

'I'll send someone with some bread for you. It wouldn't do having you arrive before the Dark Lord looking like starving waifs'.

Before long they were on the move again. Mitchell was strapped to Aislinn's back with a piece of cloth and for the time being he was content. 'Mama, Papa?' he asked in his limited vocabulary, 'I want Mama.'

'I know you miss them Mitchell, but they are visiting the Great One at the moment and I'm here to look after you now.'

It was easier to pretend they were away than trying to explain the truth to him right now. Soon enough he would realize they were on their own. Maddy cried softly to herself, her little lip quivering as her salty tears left grubby streaks down her sooty face. She clutched her little doll that Grandma had made, grateful that Struan had thought to grab it when they had escaped the burning home. Struan knew how precious it was to her, and how she drew comfort from it while sleeping each night. It was the only possession they had left from their life at the cottage, so in some ways it was precious to each of them for different reasons.

Aislinn whispered to them as they walked slowly through the bleak landscape, 'We are champions, winners, favoured, we are Hamilton's – remember the Great One is with us.'

She was careful the men did not hear her, as she was certain that they would be annoyed, but she was also determined they would not be bewitched by the Dark Lord.

The terrain was rough and unforgiving and they needed to rest often. Thick mist rolled over the moors playing hide and seek with them, slowing them further.

Aislinn begged the young man she assumed had challenged the cloaked man.

'Please,' have pity on my little brother and sister. They can't walk another step - they're exhausted!'

He looked at her blankly and then a flicker of sympathy registered in his eyes.

'I'll see what I can do about getting them a seat in the cart'

Soon the children were settled into the supply cart for their limbs were too leaden to move any longer. They slept erratically and dreamed of days when laughter and joy filled their lives intermingled with dark creatures that snatched them from this happiness. The last time they had travelled in a cart was when they had embarked on their adventure to find Griswold.

⌘

Mackenzie Hamilton and Imogene, together with their three children had left their Homeland with the clothes on their backs, a trunk of clothing, linen and a wagon drawn by one horse. They owned nothing else but the dreams of a new life in Griswold. Although they had given up all they had, they did not feel burdened by the task before them. They eagerly anticipated their new life and found the adventure they were starting exhilarating. That journey had taken them three months and was arduous. The combination of slow travel, a weary horse, the forces of nature and needing new supplies presented daily challenges for them. Eventually they reached the place that Imogene had seen in her dreams one night. This was a place where hope had been lost and where the Dark Lord's powers had become evident – located deep in the heart of Griswold. The land was beautiful if you looked at it with your natural eye, but if you perceived it with your heart and soul it was a superficial beauty that was not lasting. This was where the Great One needed them. They bought a small piece of land with money the Elders had given them before they left. There they set up a home building their stone cottage with a thatch roof. The same cottage that was now a pile of burnt stones and smouldering rubble!

'Thank goodness for your family thatching experience,' Imogene had teased Mac. 'Some inherited family skills are helpful,' she giggled as they had bundled the straw together.

So in time they had established themselves in the community, and they were well loved by the people. Imogene cared for families by providing meals when needed, for the ill with basic herbal medicines and the children by teaching basic reading and writing skills. Mac would spend hours talking to the Great One, inquiring of Him how to help the people. Although he never experienced the Great One as in his childhood, he felt sure he whispered mysteries to him and showed him what he needed to teach those around him. It was a good and satisfying life for the family, so they believed.

Griswold had not always been such a wasteland. It was once a paradise before the Dark Lord had made his home there. It swarmed with living creatures of every kind and the air had been sustaining. There was never drought and the trees produced fruit all year round. Strange mythical creatures like unicorns had been found in the land and there was a peace that presided over the country at that time.

All that had changed when the Dark Lord invaded this paradise and taught the people living there about distrust, deceit and war. He bewitched them so that each man would think only of himself and his needs, and so selfishness was born. Unicorns fled to hide in the forests and could no longer be part of the landscape as people began to hunt them for their horns which they believed had healing powers. No one was completely safe anymore in Griswold. Paradise was a dream of the past.

The Hamilton's noticed this change in Griswold as the years passed – the lifeless land and forests devoid of beautiful creatures and plants. It was dying little by little, everywhere except their piece of farmland. It miraculously flourished and produced healthy crops, the weeping willow growing tall and strong year after year, the Great One's goodness and favour evident to them all.

## CHAPTER 2
# FEAR

*Fear makes us feel our humanity*
— Benjamin Disraeli

THE CAVE was dark, hidden deep in the hills of Griswold, Two bodies lay huddled together and the air crackled with burning twigs as firelight danced around the stony cave walls. Someone watched the figures from the dark recesses of the cave walls – watching and waiting.

⌘

Night fell and the cart carrying the children climbed up the steep hill toward the dark castle that lay perched at the top. It was eerily etched against the skyline like a crooked, evil hand ready to snatch up those who passed, never to be seen again. The children were hungry and tired and Mitchell whimpered quietly against Aislinn's chest. He had cried earlier in the day when the cloaked man had yelled at him and threatened him with his sword.

'I'll cut out that tongue of yours, and then we'll see just how much noise you'll make.' Mitchell had whimpered and sought comfort from his sister.

'Shh Mitchell, don't be scared. I'm here to look after you. I won't let anyone hurt you.'

She whispered soothingly in his ear, glaring at the cloaked man with contempt in her eyes. *How could he be so mean to such a little boy?* Mitchell snuggled closer to his sister drawing comfort from her. They had always had a very close bond and he trusted her implicitly.

Maddy and Struan curled up together in the corner of the cart, pretending they were on an adventure. It was their way of keeping up their spirits, pretending they were exploring new and exciting places.

'Whatever happens,' whispered Aislinn, 'do not look the Dark Lord in the eyes. We don't want to be bewitched by him. We have to stick together.'

They all agreed that they would do everything in their power to stay true to the values their parents had taught them.

The men shouted and cheered as they approached the castle - clearly they were delighted to be home. What brought them happiness as they passed through the arch brought fear and unease to the children. The large, creaking gate opened, reminding Aislinn that their freedom was at an end. She felt a little hope in her heart waver. They were now at the mercy of the Dark Lord – at the very centre of Griswold's evil.

⌘

The sleeping man stretched slowly, then sat up startled, unsure of his surroundings He looked around, wild-eyed. He saw his companion lying beside him in the dark cave. How did they get here? Soft fur pelts formed a bed for them and a warm fire glowed and crackled beside them sending sparks into the air every now and again. At his stirring, his companion roused from deep sleep and looked around equally confused as he. It took them a few moments to adjust their eyes and for reality to sink in.

The large man who had been watching them stepped out from the shadows of the cave startling them. He was huge, his form filling the mouth of the cave, leaving them no escape route. His chiselled body reminded them of a warrior, but it was his eyes that captivated them – even in the dim firelight he could see into your soul. Around him was an electric charge that was both powerful and frightening.

'I am Nuada,' he said, his deep voice echoing through the cave. 'I have been sent to protect and watch over you as you journey on.'

'Who sent you?' the man asked - suspicious, unsure.

'The Great One.'

Relief settled upon them both at the name spoken – they would be safe now.

'He has a special for task for you.'

⌘

The children were bundled into a tower room of the castle, which Aislinn assumed was just a little better than the dungeons. The room was not very large and contained a bed, a small table and two chairs and a chamber pot. The strong metal bars across the windows reinforced the fact that they were now prisoners of the Dark Lord and trapped in a situation that seemed impossible. Aislinn carefully laid little Mitchell down on the bed and covered him with the threadbare blanket that was folded at the bottom of the bed. He looked afraid and bewildered by all that had taken place. Softly she sang a song to him in her beautiful voice, soothing away his fears. Struan and Maddy explored the little room, which did not take long.

'How are we going to get out of here?' Struan asked although he expected no answer to the impossible question.

'We can escape whenever we want to,' said Maddy earnestly.

'Don't be silly Maddy,' Struan scoffed, a little annoyed at his sisters stupid comment. He was tired of playing pretend games – it got them nowhere and he had humoured her enough – she needed a reality check.

'It's true,' she retorted boldly standing her ground. 'Papa says that whenever we use our imagination we can go to many places and enjoy them as if we were really there,' Maddy persisted, desperately needing a ray of hope to cling to.

'Papa doesn't know everything Maddy. He said we would have a good life if we fulfilled the Prophecies and look where that got us,' Struan spat out meanly.

Maddy's eyes welled with tears, the reminder of her parents' death raw.

'Stop it! There's no point arguing - we need to work together and make sure we keep our strength and our spirits up,' Aislinn reminded them. 'The most important thing is to stay together and keep one another encouraged. Papa did say that hope and faith are two of the most important things in overcoming hard times - and our imagination, Maddy,' she added fondly for the benefit of her sister. 'Whenever one of us is sad or losing heart, then the rest of us need to be strong. We need faith to see, hope to dream and love to be...'

The use of this expression reminded them of their aching hearts– Mama often used this expression and it was one that had become a family joke and eventually the family motto, but there was truth in it – they would need faith, hope and love to see them through this mess.

Aislinn kept her fears of the Dark Lord's plans to herself - she did not want her siblings losing courage. She knew after eavesdropping on the cloaked man's argument that he was going to try and entice them into his kingdom. She had heard the tales that he could be charming and winsome. That was part of his deceptive and lying nature. Papa had told her all about it - how he had convinced many people to rally to his kingdom with persuasive words, subtle deeds and promises of things he never delivered on.

'Don't ever believe him, Aislinn,' Papa had said. 'He will promise you the world for your allegiance, but will suck the very life out of you when you follow him. He does not know of love, joy and peace and the only person he cares about is himself and his own power and prestige.'

Somehow, Aislinn would have to remind her siblings of his nature without terrifying them more. But that would come in time. For now, she needed to trust in the Great One and whisper words to Him to encourage herself for the battle that was certain to come. She thought of her parents and hoped that the Great One had welcomed them home with the love and honour they deserved. She missed them and knew that the days to come would be tough for them all. She was all her siblings had left. They would never know the love of their mother and father ever again.

⌘

The two cave-dwellers eyed the warrior standing before them, questions written all over their faces. He smiled reassuringly at them.

'It's true' he laughed, 'you really are here.'

The man looked at his companion and then at his body. This was incredible – he felt so good – there was no way he could be in this condition – the times they lived in had caused this – his blood had flowed furiously. He remembered leaving his body – the shell that had housed him for the last thirty-eight years. He lifted his shirt which he noticed was clean and crisp – not the one he had previously been wearing. He gasped, running his hand over the scar that stretched across his body. The wound was pink but perfectly healed- a reminder of all he had endured. This was not possible.

His companion was equally dumbstruck. She had seen him die before she blacked out.

'I remember now!' the man exclaimed.

'Welcome back Mac,' Nuada said hugging him fiercely.

The cruel blow from the cloaked man's sword had indeed cut through his midriff, and as he fell to the ground his life flashing before him, a miraculous thing had happened. He left his body, floating up from the world as he knew it, finding himself before the Great One again – just like his childhood. The Great One had embraced him in his huge arms and as he hugged Mac he breathed life back into him, whispering, 'Your enemies are my enemies. Your time is not up and although you have tasted death I will let you rise again and be stronger than ever before. Your task is to find that which was stolen from you by the Dark Lord, and retrieve it. As you do you will discover your true purpose in this life. It will all make sense Mac when you find yourself again. I have granted Imogene life too, as you will need to take down the Dark Lord together – there is greater strength in your unity than you can imagine.'

He had never felt such peace before – he wanted to cry out, beg to be allowed to stay in this glorious place, but before he could, he had drifted back to his body on the dusty ground. Imogene had been left for dead swinging from the old, gnarly weeping willow tree. What the warriors had failed to notice as they rode away was the man who stepped from behind the tree cutting her down gently, breathing life back into her still form.

Imogene at last found her voice.

'The children, where are our children?' she asked dreading his answer. 'Are they dead?

Before Nuada could answer Mac punched his fist into the air. 'That's it!' he shouted.

'The children are alive - the Dark Lord has stolen them from us. That's what the Great One meant when he told me to recover what was stolen – it's our children Imogene!'

Nuada nodded in agreement then continued, 'There's more that you need to recover – your children are only a part of what was stolen from you – the Dark Lord has something else that belongs to you.'

They looked at him – confused and alarmed – everything they owned was burned up in the fire.

'Come with me,' he said.

# Chapter 3

# Identity

*We know what we are, but not what we may be*

— William Shakespeare

AISLINN sang and Maddy joined in, their sweet voices filling the tower with the presence of the Great One. It was comforting to the children for they could feel his closeness. The presence of love, goodness and purity was so opposite to the usual presence that filled the Dark Lord's castle and the ground literally shook, the earth at war with itself.

The Dark Lord was well aware that the Great One's presence was being summoned in the castle tower and he was furious. This was his domain - how dare the Great One enter it. He felt powerless which stoked his anger more, as power was the one thing he desired above all else. He ordered his witches and wizards immediately to his chamber to see what could be done to eradicate this awful presence of goodness from his castle.

'What's the meaning of this presence? I thought you had cast your spells to place an impenetrable barrier around my castle?'

'We did Master,' a small, rather unusual looking wizard replied. 'We followed all the spells we know to protect you. Your welfare is of great concern to us, for without you we have nothing. The problem is that the Great One is the creator of all power and what we have is limited in comparison.'

'Wrong answer you insolent creature! The brutal slap across the ear left the little wizard cowering in fear.

'Make every effort to neutralize him in my castle. I won't tolerate his presence here. Now get out – you're only as important in my life as I allow you to be,' he threatened menacingly. 'I gave you your power and I can take it back,' he spat.

He paced up and down his chamber after they left. The Great One's presence always left him unnerved and fearful, but this was not something his subjects should see. They had to believe he was as powerful as he professed otherwise he would lose everything. They followed him out of fear and dread and as long as he could make them believe they were on the winning side and that the world would belong to them soon, they would continue to serve him. They must never see the goodness of the Great One or all would be lost!

The Dark Lord had a secret and he feared that if it ever came out he would be ruined. Many years before, he had been the Great One's closest advisor and confidant. He had been known by his name Sephtis then. How he hated that name, almost as much as the woman who had given it to him. She had not loved him but blamed him for her hardship and cursed the day he was ever born to her. His father had chosen to abandon her, leaving her alone and pregnant and he had borne the brunt of her hatred and bitterness. She had named him Sephtis which means eternal death. Well he had certainly lived up to her prediction, for every time he was called by that name he felt a little more of his soul die within, a little more eaten by jealousy and envy. The Great One had never judged him but always believed that he could achieve more than his mother ever believed. He had continually told Sephtis that his name did not have to define him. He had seen the many wonderful things the Great One had done and how he cared and loved the people of the land. Sephtis had tried his very best to work as hard as he could for the Great One – to make him proud. He desperately wanted to be recognized and elevated to a position of authority and power – to become someone great and prove his mother wrong. What infuriated him the most though, was that no matter how hard he tried or worked he was always treated with equal favour and love as everyone else in the Great One's kingdom, even those who did nothing and were not worthy of any rewards in his eyes.

This jealousy and desperation to be recognized had brewed and boiled in his heart and mind till he began to believe that he should be favoured. Finally he became so envious of the Great One's power that he had attempted to overthrow him.

Sephtis had learned firsthand about betrayal – his deceitful plot was uncovered but even then the Great One remained calm and gracious offering him the opportunity for redemption. His pride and bitterness had not allowed him to accept this offer he had left the Great One's kingdom to begin life afresh elsewhere – to set up his own kingdom and rule. That was when he discovered Griswold, but he never forgot his humiliation or his desire to make the Great One pay. Yes, Sephtis was dead and he had to make sure that he remained so. He had been reborn as Legion in the hope of leading many men but he quickly became known as the Dark Lord amongst the people of Griswold, and he would rule as such.

⌘

The children ate hungrily when their dinner arrived as they were famished after their long journey with little nourishment. Aislinn and Struan were surprised at how good the food was. They expected a watery gruel that all prisoners received, but instead they had choice roast meat with vegetables and even some sweet treats. Aislinn was instantly suspicious of this generosity as she knew that the Dark Lord did not have a generous bone in his body. She was correct in thinking he was trying to curry favour with them before he met them. He had decided on the strategy of being charming- his plan was to seduce the children with kindness instead of having them fear him. He knew that Mackenzie and Imogene would have schooled their children well and if they feared him, he would never win their trust. For now, it would be in his best interest to treat them well. Everything within his nature struggled to be kind, as he was filled with hatred, but the end result of using the children's gifts for the destruction of others and the Great One enabled him to hide his evil side in a disguise of light.

The children felt drained emotionally and physically and Aislinn helped the younger ones wash their faces and weary bodies with the jug of water that had been provided. They had each received a new set of clothing which they gratefully put on, being glad to remove their dusty, smoky clothing – the last remnants of that awful night. If only their memories could be changed as easily as their clothing. Then she sat them on the bed and they began to speak to the Great One. They shared their fears and grief and asked for his help. Struan however held back his emotion, remaining silent and withdrawn. The weight of responsibility of being the man of the family rested heavily upon him and he wondered if he would ever have the courage and the conviction of his father. He did not want to disappoint Papa and Mama or the Great One, but at the same time he couldn't help the intense, seething anger he felt. He was angry with his parents for bringing them to this miserable land; furious with them for leaving, even though his mind told him they had no choice in the matter but most of all he was angry with the Great One for deserting them in their time of trouble. If the Great One loved them as much as Papa said he did, then why had he allowed this to happen? Hadn't they always been taught by Papa that the Great One was good – that he protected the ones he loved? These questions plagued his thoughts and he could find no answer to them.

Struan had no idea that the Great One was watching him, lovingly and tenderly. He was unaware that Great One had a plan, and most of all, he had no idea that through this trial he would discover things about himself and the Great One he had never known.

⌘

In the midnight hour, when all was quiet, Aislinn was woken by a presence in their room. She was not sure if she were dreaming or whether she was awake. Fear overwhelmed her and her body froze - *the Dark Lord had come to bewitch them.*

'Don't be afraid,' whispered the voice sensing her terror. 'The Great One sent us to deliver a message to you. He wants you to know that we will be around to keep you from harm while you are here.'

'What do you mean by us? Who are you?'

'I am Ryder, Protector of the Innocent.'

He stepped out from the shadows, his tunic the most pure and translucent Aislinn had ever seen. It wasn't white or silver, but a shimmering mother of pearl colour. His hair flowed down to his shoulders and he had wings with beautiful, soft feathers on his back. He stood seven foot tall with a sword on his belt.

Suddenly she was aware of another person in the room. It was a woman wearing a dress of rainbow colours that cascaded to the floor in shimmering waves. In answer to Aislinn's questioning gasp she softly spoke, her words like that of sweet honey.

'I'm Serena, Protector of Gifts given to you. The Great One has many gifts – some you already have, and some he has yet to give to you.'

She was the most beautiful woman Aislinn had ever seen, with long fair hair the colour of spun gold, flowing down to her waist. Her hair was caught back in the front with what looked like jewels beaded into a plait.

A third person stepped from the shadows, his skin so dark, ebony in the moonlight. He was tall and regal, cloaked in a striking purple tunic with a golden sash. He smiled at Aislinn, his white teeth gleaming in his dark face. She liked him immediately.

'Hello Aislinn – I'm Regent, Protector of Royalty.' He bowed gallantly.

'But...' she stammered, convinced this must be a sweet dream; 'we're not royalty. Why are you here?'

Regent laughed, deep and rumbling from his belly, reminding Aislinn of her father's laugh which somehow comforted her yet left an indescribable ache in the pit of her stomach at the same time.

'You certainly are royalty,' he said smiling at her confused expression. 'Everyone's royal. Royalty is not just a lineage of birthright but its understanding that we are all special and unique. Most people just don't know it. I've come to make sure that you understand who you really are because the Dark Lord will try to steal that from you. You have to know who you are to overcome him Aislinn – it's the only way.'

She felt so overwhelmed that she blinked a few times, convinced that when she looked up again they would be gone and she would awaken from this beautiful dream.

'This can't be happening, I must be dreaming,' she muttered to herself, shaking her head side to side.

They were still there smiling at her and slowly it dawned on her that this was a real encounter – the kind Papa had told her about. Her desire to experience the Great One like her Papa had, was now her reality and her heart leapt in her chest. Serena clasped her hands. Aislinn felt something hard and cold fill the palm of her hand. She looked down to see the most beautiful jewel she had ever seen. It was large, about the size of small pebble, an exquisite gleaming purple.

'This will remind you that beautiful gifts come from the Great One.'

Before Aislinn could reply, Regent's huge hands engulfed her tiny hands. Instantly they were covered in shimmering, golden dust. She stared in wonder, more and more gold appearing on her sparkling hands. She looked inquiringly at him and he laughed.

'This confirms you are royalty and that goodness is in you. That gold comes from within you Aislinn. It is not something that comes from outside.'

As Ryder stepped forward, a beautiful, soft white feather floated from his wings and rested on her shoulder.

'My turn now Aislinn - this feather is my gift to you – it may not seem like much after a jewel or gold dust but guard it with all you're worth. This is a symbol of purity and is also within you - There are those who would do anything to steal it from you. Having this is a great gift – everything done in life with a pure heart is always a good thing and will help you to make the right choices. We'll always be with you, but you won't always see us as we are in battle with the Dark Lord and can only show ourselves when it is safe for you.'

'Why can't you take us with you,' Aislinn asked, hopefully.

'We wish we could, but this is a battle that must be won by you – only your victory against the Dark Lord will truly set you free. Take courage, be strong – we'll be back again soon.'

With that the room returned to the way it was. The moonlight shone through the bars of the window and although it was cold, Aislinn felt warmth stirring in her heart. For the first time since the attack she felt safe and protected. It was going to be all right. She looked again at the beautiful gem in her hand and the soft white feather. They may not have a father and mother anymore, but they had family – The Great One had heard their cries. She tucked her treasures inside the pillowcase where they would be safe and curled up next to Mitchell. Despite her uncertainty for the future she slept soundly for the first time, secure in the knowledge they were being protected.

# Chapter 4

# Betrayal

*Everyone suffers at least one bad betrayal in their lifetime. It's what unites us. The trick is not to let it destroy your trust in others when that happens. Don't let them take that from you*

— Sherrilyn Kenyon, Invincible

'How will we rescue the children and this mysterious thing stolen from us? We don't even know what the other thing is' Imogene asked Mac.

They still felt weak after the attack that had come.

'I have no idea, but I guess the fact that the Great One has chosen to give us life again when it was snatched away must mean he has a plan for us to follow. We'll do whatever he shows us to. More than anything I trust my life to him.'

Before, they had felt confident in their abilities the Great One had given them, but now they had no idea how to proceed. The details of the attack were vague and unclear to them. It had happened so fast and the memories were a blur. Somehow the numbness was comforting, but that would not see them through or give them the will to fight this battle. The Great One knew this. He had seen many before them give up all hope and faith when they were hurt and betrayed. Many had failed as a result of shame causing them to retreat into their shells - he did not want this for Mackenzie and Imogene Hamilton.

Nuada led them deeper into the cave, lighting the way for them as they ventured deep within the mountain's belly.

'The Great One wants to show you the events of that night again. He wants you to see the details and who was involved in the attack. I assure you, this is not to hurt you but to help you understand many things. His desire is for you to rise from the ashes of pain; to pursue the future, but to do that you have to let go of the past.

Tears pooled in Imogene's eyes and slowly rolled down her cheeks - her heart ached at the thought.

'I don't want to see what those savages did to us.'

The force of her anger surprised Mac, who knew her as a sweet and tender woman – they had stolen her sweetness too. He held her in his arms, understanding her pain as he too was wrestling with similar emotions and agony. He also felt incredible rage deep down at having his life stolen and his family shattered. Still worse, he did not understand why it had happened. Maybe this would give them some answers.

'That is your choice,' Nuada said, 'but I warn you that the decision you make now will have repercussions for your whole family.'

Mac stroked his wife gently nodding at Nuada. They had four children who needed them and there was no place for their emotions to get in the way now. No matter how painful this would be, they needed to do it.

'We'll do what we must to make this right,' he whispered.

As if by magic the one side of the cave wall lit up, alive as if in motion. There before them they could see a vision of their little farmhouse in the dead of night. Everything looked peaceful, the clouds making pictures across their roof as the moon teased them. Then from the shadows crept the hooded men circling their home and torching the roof. There were eight in all and in the firelight of the burning walls the cloaked man's face became visible to Mac and Imogene.

'No it can't be true!' Mac groaned.

It was Cillian - one of their most trusted leaders and friends.

'How can this be,' Imogene wept distraught, the closeness of the betrayal suffocating her. 'I can't believe it was him. Why would he do this to us?'

The question remained unanswered. It was betrayal of the worst kind. One by one each of the men's faces were revealed in the firelight, each a fresh stab wound to their hearts. They knew them all – men they had loved and worked with – people they saw as friends. The final betrayal played out as Cillian took his sword and slashed Mac across his midriff, leaving him to fall to the ground in a lifeless heap, commanding Imogene to be hung from the nearby tree. They watched the vision as the men rode away with their heartbroken children, with not a care at what they had done to their family.

The agony of what they had just seen cut so deep and numerous emotions passed through them as they tried to process the vision, but words failed them. They felt pain, betrayal, rejection and grief; then anger started to bubble in their hearts leaving an unfamiliar taste of bitterness. They had no time to allow it to settle however, as another scenario flashed up on the cave wall.

This showed their family a few months before the attack, going about their daily lives, training up followers for the Great One, loving those who needed it. Before they could wonder where this vision was going, the picture changed. Being one of the few families to harvest bountiful crops on their fertile piece of land came with a price. The responsibility they felt for others had worn them out and as a result they sometimes neglected to perceive what families needed at certain times. This had caused a seed of mistrust and criticism to enter the community. Slowly the penny dropped as Mac and Imogene gazed at the whole picture – things had changed when their community had moved from being caring and loving to a community who gathered only for the weekly supplies. People no longer loved them for who they were, but for what supplies they could get from them. When the supplies weren't enough, criticism followed causing mutual trust and love to be eroded slowly over time, so subtly that no one noticed. It was further fuelled by servants of the Dark Lord's ranks meddling and promising fame and wealth to those who fuelled this criticism. Mutual honour and respect then quickly evaporated.

'We're sorry Great One. We should have been aware of what was happening around us – we should have known better and led more wisely. If we had not focused on providing supplies but rather on love we would not have made these mistakes. We should have taught them to care for themselves and not to rely on us as their provision.'

Nuada broke into their sorrow. Their pain was evident, self-recrimination the punishment they carried.

'Don't go down that road - he is not disappointed with you. He loves you too much to let you die striving to be something he never called you to be. That is why you must find the treasure that was stolen from you.'

Mac and Imogene still did not understand what he was saying.

'How do we forgive those who betrayed us?' Mac asked in a broken voice. 'How do we forgive ourselves for the mess we've made?'

'Betrayal works two ways, as you have seen. You have been betrayed and you have betrayed others unknowingly. It won't be the first or the last time it will happen. What you do with it is determined by how you respond to it.' Nuada left the sentence hanging – the decision was theirs to make.

The cave wall lit up again, revealing another picture. It showed Cillian and his family and how they were hurt by Mac and Imogene during a difficult time in their lives. An old man lay on a bed, clearly his life coming to an end. His family waited and watched over him, their pain evident. Imogene brought meals and Mac visited on occasion trying to encourage the family as best he knew how. They thought they were showing their care, but expectations are a strange thing. Unless they are made known, they can be misinterpreted as was the case here. Cillian felt abandoned in his time of pain by Mac and Imogene. It was these unfulfilled expectations that bred bitterness and prompted him to write all his grievances into a document that stretched on in what seemed like a never-ending scroll. The Elders would hear of Mac and Imogene's thoughtlessness. In his mind they did not deserve to lead the people. He further plotted by stirring up others with gossip and discussions of what should be done about Mackenzie and Imogene.

'They don't deserve to be our leaders- they don't really care about us. When was the last time they visited you or helped you with food supplies?' were the questions bandied about, a deadly community, poisoning people wherever it found a heart to root itself. It grew with silent maliciousness until it was eventually believed by all who heard it. The tree of bitterness had taken root - its fruit would bring nothing but destruction.

'A little poison goes a long way,' Nuada said meaningfully. 'It is not the kind of poison you want to savour.'

Mac's anger faded as fast as it had erupted together with the pictures on the cave wall. He understood Nuada. It was for their redemption to see what had transpired. Yes, the hurt was deep and painful – betrayal always painfully cruel but they had choices to make about what to do now. They had to forgive despite their heartbreak – he knew they had no choice, but would Imogene be able to do it so soon after being betrayed?

'Imogene, sweetheart, we have to let this go - if we don't it will devour us and we'll become the very thing we've just seen played out –bitter and vengeful - something we don't want to be. Our hearts will harden and we won't ever be able to trust or love others again. Worse, we won't be able to save our children and be the parents they need.'

'I know you are right Mac, but it's so hard. People we trusted and loved as our own flesh and blood have betrayed us in the most horrible way. How do you forget that? It's more than that too. Not only did Cillian betray us but he hates us so much that he even wanted us dead. He was willing to let our children become orphans because of his hatred and anger. That is what is so hard to forgive.'

'You're right Imogene but if we become as bitter as he is then we are no better. The Great One has shown us that justice prevails – he rescued us from an evil so consuming and is giving us another chance to do the right thing. I for one don't want to throw that away because my heart and pride is wounded. Besides, we made mistakes too – we messed up and didn't see what was really needed in our community – we have to take responsibility for our part in this mess too. There's also a difference between forgiving and forgetting Imogene. No-one expects us to forget the heartbreak we have endured but even in that place of pain it is possible to forgive those who hurt us.'

'Forgiveness is never about a feeling but rather about a choice you make,' Nuada interjected. 'Your anger and hurt are valid feelings Imogene, but they don't have to stop you forgiving.'

She knew he was right and that they had other things to concentrate on – getting their children back was their first priority. They had no time to wallow in self-pity. She nodded and Mac smiled weakly at her, relief flooding his face. He was always amazed how strong she could be. They also both knew that this wasn't over though – that in the weeks and months down the road they would have to return to their emotions and face them – that forgiveness would be a journey and not just a destination, a choice made every day, and some days would be harder than others.

Mac turned and faced Nuada.

'We're sorry – I realize how insensitive and full of pride we were. Can he forgive us for our mistakes? We will forgive them for what they have done – they will have their own journey and demons to work through.'

Knowing the truth and gaining some understanding of the attack brought them a measure of freedom again. There would certainly be times when forgiving themselves and those who put them here would be hard to do, but the Great One knew it would come in time. Nuada beamed at them. 'You are like bears in a cave. You will have a short time of rest here and healing of your hearts, but when you leave this cave you will be fierce contenders – strong and sure of yourselves again.'

'I hope so.'

'You will,' he promised them.

Mac and Imogene walked back to the entrance of the cave arm in arm. A ray of sunlight pierced through the trees in dancing light. The smell of the fresh morning filled their nostrils with hope. Mac felt so grateful – they had been given a second chance at their lives. They would be reunited as a family again – he was sure of it. He still had so many questions to ask, but for now he was content to trust the Great One to restore them and to protect his beloved children. He thought of them with longing in his heart and a prayer on his tongue.

## CHAPTER 5

# TREACHERY

*Destiny is a good thing to accept when it's going your way. When it isn't, don't call it destiny; call it injustice, treachery, or simple bad luck*

— Joseph Heller

LEGION paced restlessly - patience had never been his strong point. He knew the Great One would never give up the Hamilton children without a fight. More than anything he wished he knew what the Great One was planning. He called his subjects to his chamber for a briefing of the events to take place. Slowly they filled the chamber - row upon row of creatures. They were all different in appearance but every single one of them omitted evil of the worst kind. There was no unity amongst his ranks. They submitted to him out of selfish gain and absolute fear. Each one jostled and pushed to be first in the chamber but then stood with wide fearful eyes when they were positioned in front of him. The stench of evil and death permeated the room, seeping from every pore in their disfigured bodies. It was like being in hell itself.

One of the most powerful creatures, the Monwing, had enormous eagle-like wings and talons that could rip you to shreds. Its body and face resembled a monkey, its powerful tail a deadly weapon. The Firegoblins, with their sulphuric yellow eyes and gaping mouths could frighten even the fearless. Some of the creatures looked quite beautiful on the outside, but when they opened their eyes or mouth, it was like something putrid was released. Then there were the usual witches and wizards in the chamber, all of different ages and abilities.

'Let me through,' shrieked a voice from between the squashed ranks. It was the voice of Mischief, one of the smaller goblins.

'Wait your turn and stop pushing,' replied Confusion, another of Legion's subjects.

As they squabbled among themselves the noise of shrieking and arguing filled the chamber, a cacophony of sound that reached an unbearable pitch.

'Enough!' roared Legion. 'You are squabbling worse than children. We are here to develop a strategy for dealing with the Hamilton children, and ultimately the Great One. More than anything I want to see him defeated once and for all.'

'I know,' shouted Confusion in eager anticipation. 'Send me out to bring confusion to the army of the Great One. While they are confused then we can attack them. No one causes confusion quite like me,' he boasted. He was really pleased with his plan of action and made a point of gloating to the creature next to him.

'No, that won't do.' said Untruth. 'We need to get them to believe the worst about the Great One then they will lose faith in his abilities and goodness and follow you Master. I am very good at spreading lies.'

The competition was on. Each creature tried to outdo the next in an attempt to gain the Master's favour. This was the usual routine of their strategic meetings and Legion was bored with it.

'We have tried all these ploys unsuccessfully in the past,' Legion reminded them. 'We need a plan that will touch his soft, caring side so he will surrender to us in defeat.'

A very small, insignificant subject crept forward, shaking, petrified. He had a plan, but he was so used to the master's wrath that he was afraid to share it. It was only the need for recognition that finally won over his fear. He was Rejection and he stammered nervously as he spoke.

'E...e...excuse me M...m...master, we have the Hamilton children here and we could hold them for ransom.'

Legion roared with laughter and in response all the other creatures began to guffaw and ridicule Rejection, causing him to shrink in humiliation.

'Why on earth would I want wealth in return for the Hamilton children you idiot? I don't want wealth, I want power! When I have power, wealth will naturally follow. The two go hand in hand.'

Rejection recoiled at his rebuke, but he knew his plan was good so he persevered.

'Master, I wasn't referring to exchanging them for wealth, but to exchanging them for something that is exceedingly precious to the Great One and will devastate him forever. He is one who loves too greatly and cannot bear to see his followers suffer. If we exchange them for his most precious possession then we may cripple him forever. Maybe he will even exchange his power for the children.'

Rejection started to doubt his plan and wished he hadn't spoken up. Why did he never learn? The Master would only embarrass him again in front of the others. Legion looked at Rejection with something akin to admiration, but it was only fleeting - he never affirmed his followers as that would show kindness and loyalty and he displayed none of those characteristics.

'Now that may be worth considering,' he said thoughtfully. 'He will never exchange his power as he cannot be separated from it –they are one and the same. I have yet to discover a way to kill him. Perhaps you're right Rejection – we need leverage. I shall make this a challenge for you and send all of you through the kingdom to discover what is so precious to the Great One. The one who can discover what that is will be richly rewarded. I want an answer yesterday and don't come back without something worthy to share. There must be something – everyone has a weakness somewhere. Find his weakness!'

There was much excitement as groups of evil creatures left the castle on the mission. They covered the skies and land of Griswold, a blanket of darkness swarming and swooping, hiding in nooks and crannies in villages and towns, their eyes and ears looking and listening for that one nugget of information they sought. Each dreamed of their rise to greatness in the Dark Lord's kingdom and each hungered for greater power.

⌘

While his subjects fought for the prize, Legion thought of the Great One and how this could cripple him if he found something of value. He hoped more than anything they would find something and show the Great One what treachery was like firsthand. He would deceive the old fool and take everything precious from him if it was the last thing he ever did.

## CHAPTER 6
# DESTINY

*It is not in the stars to hold our destiny but in ourselves*

— William Shakespeare

MAC and Imogene left the cave with Nuada after they were fully rested. They travelled for a couple of days with no idea where their destination was - they had to trust Nuada to direct them on their journey. He had clear instructions from the Great One where to lead them.

'This will be a place like no other you have ever experienced, but you are ready to see it now. It will help you to understand what was stolen from you and how to get it back.'

To Mac and Imogene, Nuada was speaking in riddles again and they glanced at each other; questions written all over their faces.

The journey was tiring, but sheer determination kept them focused on the task. Imogene desperately missed her children and reaching them was the only thing on her mind. She would travel to the centre of the earth if that's what it took to see them again.

They heard the thundering waterfall before they saw it. It cascaded down the rock face sending a fine mist into the air. It was both beautiful and powerful at the same time. Mac rushed to the crystal clear water scooping it into his mouth thirstily. He then splashed his face savouring the cool, refreshing feeling.

'It's amazing,' Imogene gasped kneeling down beside him as she scooped up water.

'Not nearly as beautiful as the place we are going,' Nuada said matter-of-factly.

'Come, we can't stop now- we're almost there. We need to pass through the falls.'

'How on earth are we going to do that?' Imogene cried looking at the powerful water as it cascaded down the cliff face in a furious sheet.

'Don't look with your natural eyes Imogene, but with faith in your heart believe that you can access places that seem impossible.'

He smiled at the look of complete confusion on her face. *They just didn't get it, but they would soon enough.*

'We'll follow your lead Nuada, but I hope you know what you are doing?'

'Have a little faith Mac,' he chuckled seeing their consternation. 'We didn't save you just to drown you in a waterfall,' he teased.

'You're telling me we need faith on this one,' Imogene muttered under her breath.

They felt the cool spray and mist of the water moistening their skin as they approached the thundering falls.

'Here, hold my hand,' Nuada said reaching out. 'Now close your eyes. Imagine a doorway through the water and don't let your fear overcome you. Fear will always shut off new experiences to you. Your mind is extremely powerful in enabling you to overcome obstacles.'

This was one of the most frightening things they had experienced – it was new territory to them and they weren't quite sure how to navigate their way through it all.

The last few days seemed totally surreal and dreamlike to them. The roar of the falling water was deafening and Imogene steeled herself against her instinct to flee, pushing down the fear that wanted to overwhelm her. She closed her eyes, her brow wrinkling in concentration as she imagined a large doorway in front of her.

Just as she thought she would surely lose her balance and be swept away by the strength of the falls, the curtain of water became smooth like a sheet of glass.

'You can look now Imogene,' Nuada laughed seeing her eyes still tightly squeezed shut.

They were now able to step behind the sheet of water and into the gateway that opened before them. It was no longer part of her imagination but a real opening. Had the power of their minds really altered nature?

Their surroundings were completely different to what they imagined. They expected a dark, damp cave behind the curtain of water, yet this completely shattered their expectation. They had literally stepped into another realm or world. Everything appeared to be living in fullness. Colours were more radiant and translucent and fragrances assailed their senses with a mixture of the most beautiful smells blended together, yet separate. Trees laden with fruit of every kind lined the bubbling river that flowed beside them, its crystal water sparkling in the sunlight and the sweet melody of its water filling their ears. Imogene and Mac stared in wonder and surprise at all they saw. Birds with the most majestic colours and calls flew through the air, deer grazed peacefully in the green grass and rolling hills. It was a glorious land. Absolutely everything was full of life and more beautiful than anything they had ever seen or experienced before.

'What is this place?' She felt breathless at the magnitude of the beauty around them. It was sensory overload.

'You'll soon see,' said Nuada. 'Eat some of this fruit to strengthen you, for the fruit here gives life and strength to those who eat it and your body has taken quite a beating of late,' he smiled.

They ate the delicious sweet fruit, juice running down their chins. It was unlike anything they had ever eaten before, the sweet, juicy flavours changing as they ate.

As they travelled they passed a number of people along the way and Nuada waved as though they were long lost friends. Laughter and joy was a constant sound that floated through the air. This was real community – friendship and love were obvious – there was no pretending here and Mac and Imogene were tangibly aware of it. Nobody was too busy to wave or shout out a greeting as they passed.

'Look!' Mac exclaimed pointing at the buildings that loomed in the distance. It appeared much bigger than a village and yet did not seem impersonal or intimidating in its size and was buzzing with activity and life.

'It's amazing,' he breathed awestruck by the size of it. The beauty and peace of this place hit Mac forcefully as realization dawned. 'Nuada is it...?'

'It is Mac – it is where the Great One lives.'

'That's impossible,' he breathed deeply. 'We would have to be dead to be here, unless this has all been a dream and we are indeed dead.'

'I assure you Mac - you are far from dead. I did warn you that fear would stop you experiencing new things. Well, unbelief and ignorance also have the same effect. Since you've never believed you could come here until you died you would never have been able to experience it; that is until your eyes were opened to the possibilities of everything around you.'

'You mean everything we've been taught has been incorrect?'

'I wouldn't say incorrect, but I would say it was very much partial truth Mac. The moment a man locks his thoughts and beliefs into one thing he closes his heart to discovering more, becoming critical of anything that challenges his views. This makes learning and experiencing greater things far more difficult, if not impossible. Just because you may not understand it or have an explanation for it, doesn't mean it doesn't exist or isn't truth.'

'This is unbelievable –. Come on let's go and see it,' he urged, eager to get to the village. Nuada had just crushed all his preconceived ideas, his narrow-minded thoughts and his self-righteous beliefs – and he was delighted by it – he felt a measure of freedom he hadn't in years. That feeling of slow suffocation he had felt the last few moons was lifting.

'Slow down Mac, my legs aren't quite as long as yours,' Imogene teased pleased to see the adventurous, excited spirit of her husband returning.

It was good to see him happy and enthusiastic again. She suddenly realized that for quite a while now he had not been his exuberant self. The task and burden of leading a community had taken its toll on him.

He had heard of the place he would one day live with the Great One but this was not how he had imagined it. The Elders always spoke about this place as a fantasy wonderland and yet this had more reality to it than any of the stories he had been told. There was no golden road leading to a city of pearly gates and jewels. Rather it was solid and built of stone and the gates were made of wood and beautifully carved. On one side of the city the river they had been following opened out forming a large lake with water as smooth and clear as glass. It was a place they were completely unfamiliar with- simple and yet beautiful. Was this real? The gates swung open as they approached and the sound of music so sweet reached their ears. They heard voices calling it took them a moment to recognize that they were part of a welcome procession and that the people of this unusual place knew exactly who they were - they were celebrating their arrival.

'How do they know who we are?' Mac asked.

'Everyone here knows who you are. We have watched over you the last few years and we are so excited to have you here today.' Nuada beamed.

This was getting weirder by the minute.

Mac and Imogene felt like they were being welcomed home amidst all of the celebrations. They followed Nuada into a very long hall, its high ceilings and beautifully carved pillars impressive and majestic. At the end of the hall was another room behind large doors. They assumed it was the throne room and they found themselves being ushered in. Mac could hardly contain his excitement. The Elders always spoke about the throne room of the Great One as though it were the most sacred place of all. To their surprise they found the Great One seated at a round table in the middle of the room. *Where was his throne?*

Mac was not sure whether he was delighted that there was no throne or completely disappointed that everything they believed was false. He decided to let all his expectations go and just enjoy the experience of being in the Great One's home.

There was no pretension of grandeur here. There was no opulence or ostentatious wealth visible. Rather there was an atmosphere that this place was filled with items of comfort and sentimentality. It had the feel of a welcoming home.

Although Mac had never seen the Great One in person, he instantly recognized him from his visions and encounters he had as a young man and he fell down before him. Imogene quickly followed suit. The Great One laughed, a deep pleasurable laugh, waving them to get up.

'Come now, you don't have to be so formal. Welcome to Lionsgate. You don't have to bow- you're part of my family. There's a feast waiting for us and we need to eat and enjoy each other's company. I've waited a long time for this meeting. Come and sit at the table with me.'

Mac and Imogene were caught off guard. They never imagined they would ever meet the Great One in their lifetime, and certainly never sit and eat with him at a feast. They had always been taught that you met the Great One when you passed into the other life and only for those who believed in him. This was turning everything they had been taught upside down on its head.

They had always pictured the Great One as being rather serious, a little stern in his demeanour and yet here before them was a lively, compassionate being; nothing like they imagined. His presence alone was captivating. His silvery hair did not age him but rather made him regal and timeless in his appearance. Light emanated from every facet of his being and the sheer force of love that flowed from him was overwhelming. His strength was evident but it didn't come from his physical stature – this was an inner strength – a force that consumed his entire being. Their entire concept of reality was swiftly being challenged.

They took their seats, the reality of their situation hitting them and they began to giggle. The Great One simply smiled at their laughter – joy was contagious in this place.

'What do you fancy to eat?' he asked them noting their surprise at his question.

'What do you mean?' Mac asked.

'Well if you could have anything what would you choose?'

'I would definitely choose roast pheasant and vegetables,' Imogene said.

'Then you shall have it my dear,' he tapped the table and a plate of food appeared before Imogene as requested, the pheasant steaming and succulent, the vegetables fresh and colourful.

They both laughed in delight.

'Your turn now Mac,' he smiled clearly enjoying their delighted response.

They ate their fill of the delicious food they had selected.

'You're not quite what we expected,' Imogene blurted out without thinking as they enjoyed their sweet treats. Immediately she slapped her hand to her mouth to stop any other words from tumbling out. She had not meant to be rude – she just felt so comfortable in his presence.

The Great One could not contain his mirth seeing her discomfort.

'And what did you expect?' he asked amusement twinkling in his eyes. .

'Someone more reserved,' she stammered, mortified that she may have offended him when he had been so hospitable.

'Oh good lord,' he roared with laughter. 'I sound so boring and predictable. I hope I never become those things. I love life and everything about it. Is that what people really think of me back in your world? We'll have to change that then,' he smiled.

## CHAPTER 7
# GRACE

*Grace is not part of consciousness; it is the amount of light in our souls, not knowledge nor reason*

— Pope Francis

THEY had known that the Great One loved them, but they always believed it could only be from a distance and they were still feeling a little ashamed at their perceived failure in the little community they had lived in. Forgiving others was not the problem. Somehow they still carried the baggage of forgiving themselves for their errors upon their shoulders. In some ways it was uncomfortable, painful and exhausting carrying this load, but another part of them felt a masochistic pleasure in feeling this way. There had to be justice. Surely wrong could only be made right if there was punishment or consequences? They had always been taught that. That was a foundational truth of their clan – when you did wrong then you were disciplined so that your character could ultimately be restored and you could be made into a better more effective person. Then the Great One would be pleased with you again.

The Great One was aware of their feelings and could have instantly lifted the load from them, yet he needed them to understand and learn how to cast that weight off themselves. The beliefs that had been put upon them by their clan would kill them – he had to undo them.

'Come with me,' he said jovially 'I want you to meet someone very precious to me,'

They walked down a long corridor until they reached a beautifully carved door. Upon entering the room, they could hear the laughter of two men.

'So that's what you call winning the game? I think there was a little mischief afoot and we will need a rematch.'

'Nonsense, you just need to learn to lose graciously.'

There was no animosity between the two men as they were clearly very fond of one another even though they teased each other mercilessly. They became aware they were being watched. The younger of the two jumped up and ran to the Great One shouting in delight, embracing him with huge affection.

He looked about thirty years old and had thick, dark hair that curled onto the collar of his tunic. His liquid brown eyes were warm and inviting.

'Father, I'm so glad you are here. You need to talk to Silas about losing graciously – he thinks I was cheating.'

'Now, now you two, you need to find something else to do besides playing games all day,' The Great One chided in a most loving and teasing manner. Turning to Mac and Imogene, he introduced the young man to them.

'This is my son, Ziah. As you can see he has rather a competitive streak in him.'

The young man roared with laughter, his eyes twinkling as he did so. His charismatic personality exuded from every pore of his body.

'Yes, I do get a bit competitive at times – I'm afraid I can't help myself.'

He winked at Mac and Imogene as he said it causing them to laugh. They were really surprised to learn that the Great One had a son, but more than that, they found themselves irresistibly drawn to him. They thought they knew all about the Great One from the teachings they had received from the Elders, but they were only now discovering aspects of his family that gave them new insight and meaning and it thrilled them both.

'It's so good to see you here,' he beamed at them. 'We've waited a long time to meet you both.'

At the surprise on their faces he chuckled with glee again. 'What I mean is that Father and I have known you a long time, but it's been at a distance because of circumstances. Now you have truly seen us, it will be a more meaningful relationship for us both.'

Imogene stared, recognition dawning but not quite reaching her consciousness.

'I know you – we've met before!' She was sure of it.

'Come let's show you some of Lionsgate,' Ziah said to them. 'If I were you Silas, I would practice a little more so that the next time we play I have a little more competition.'

Silas pulled a face at him showing his disgust.

'Just wait Ziah – I will slaughter you next time,' he promised.

Lionsgate was indeed beautiful. They walked out into the gardens enjoying the warmth and gentle breeze. There was something magical about the place and it wasn't the grandeur as its simplicity gave it a charm of its own. Rather it was the atmosphere of love and acceptance for everyone that caught their attention. They were surprised to see some people that they knew from their days living in Griswold. When they had died, some of them had not believed in the Great One. Mac and Imogene had believed they had been consumed by the darkness yet here they were in Lionsgate living with the Great One, part of his family.

'I see you are wondering about some people you've seen here?' the Great one asked, as though reading their minds.

'Yes, I know some of them did not serve you and follow you when they were living in Griswold. How did they come to be here?'

'I am not the monster that people make me out to be Mac. I love people no matter what. Unconditional love is only unconditional if there are no expectations or demands placed on a person. The moment we expect people to conform to rituals or traditions we are placing conditions on that love. I don't do that. All are welcome at Lionsgate.

Again their beliefs were being confronted – their perception of reality challenged. The more they learned, the less they realized they knew about the one they followed.

Imogene walked with Ziah while Mac went on ahead with the Great One.

'Tell me,' she asked, 'where do I know you from? I know we've met before but I do not recall where.'

'Yes you have met me in a sense Imogene,' Ziah said quietly. 'It was at the willow tree on your farm.' He waited for her to remember.

'You were the one who saved me?' she asked incredulously touching the scar that surrounded her throat– a reminder of their heartache.

'I remember now – it was your face I saw – you took me down from the tree and breathed life back into me. I thought I was dreaming but it was real. Ziah, you are the one who saved my life!'

'You owe me nothing Imogene. It was my pleasure to bring you back and seeing your family reunited will be more than enough reward for me.'

She smiled, gratitude oozing from her eyes.

'You and your father are so unlike anyone I've ever met before.'

'Love is a powerful thing Imogene – it can conquer the worst kind of evil – remember that.'

'Hey you two, what are you in such deep conversation about?' Mac asked.

He had noticed the belt around Ziah's waist containing a large set of keys. They jangled as he moved and even that sounded melodious in this incredible place. The keys were solid gold and unusual in shape - very distinctive.

'What are those keys for Ziah?' he asked, curiosity finally getting the better of him.

'These keys are very important. They offer freedom in more ways than one. I am the Key Keeper in Lionsgate - the one who unlocks the way. These keys are never far from me.'

'Could they unlock freedom for my children?'

'They can unlock freedom for anyone if used correctly. Although I hold the keys as Key Keeper, I need those in captivity to cry out for freedom and to recognize they need it. When a man recognizes that he is in need of the key then he can access freedom and overcome any obstacle.'

'So it's true then that a man can only be rescued when he believes in you Ziah?' Mac asked. That is what he had been taught by the Elders of their clan about the Great One. 'Surely that is conditional love then?' he asked them. This was all so confusing.

'No you misunderstand me Mac,' Ziah smiled. 'All mankind is already rescued because the Great One loves them and has given them that gift. No one has to do anything to achieve it. The freedom I am talking about is something different and you will understand what I mean in time.'

Mac still looked confused and Ziah just laughed.

'It will come to you Mac – don't worry about it.'

'Come' said the Great One. 'It's time to show Mac and Imogene what they have come to see. They walked to a section of Lionsgate they hadn't seen which had numerous rooms. Imogene wondered how they managed to find their way around all the passages without getting lost. Somehow nothing seemed to look the same twice and was multi-dimensional. They entered a room that appeared to be a treasury although it was not overflowing with abundant wealth as one would imagine. Mac and Imogene had always believed that there would be incredible wealth in the Great One's kingdom but this seemed contrary to their belief.

'I see it's not what you expected?' he stated. 'There are incredible riches here in Lionsgate but not the kind you associate with wealth. People are the treasure here – they are the true wealth. Every person has value in this life and their presence makes it a richer place.

The Great One stopped at a golden book resting on a crystal pedestal and opened it up. There were two distinct sections to his book. In the first section, Mac and Imogene saw their names and the names of their children written in beautiful golden ink. The second section of the book contained records of deeds and feats they had accomplished and space to record their future achievements. Mac craned his neck, curious to see if anything was written about their future. The Great One looked chidingly at him.

'You won't find your future here Mac,' he said. 'You are the master of your destiny – I don't make you a slave to do my bidding – you get to choose how you enjoy life and live it out. You map out your course and there will be plenty of time for that but first you need to finish this task and find that which was stolen from you.'

He showed them what had been recorded about them up to their time in Lionsgate and they looked at him confused. They did not understand.

'Why haven't you recorded our mistakes?' Mac asked the Great One suspiciously.

'You have every detail of our life here except the errors we've made. I can only see good deeds written here.'

'I'm well aware you're not perfect Mac,' smiled the Great One, 'but I have never expected you to be. No one is perfect. The errors aren't written here because they have been taken care of through my choosing to forgive you. This is a gift I've given you – it's called grace,' he said gently.

'But why have the book then, if not to keep a record of both wrongs and rights?"

'The book is not for me to use as a weapon Mac. The book is simply to document your history, the things you have achieved. It is here to encourage people to believe in themselves and to write their own story. Unfortunately most don't get to see this book till they have passed on, and then it is too late to change their lives, but a lucky few believe that there is more to life, ask questions and seek truth for themselves. This book helps them to discover their true selves and to unlock their desires and dreams. This book is not for my benefit but for yours and everyone else.'

'So there really is nothing about our past errors?' Mac asked incredulous. He had believed that this book was the damning evidence brought against you when you faced the Great One at the end of your life.

'Unlike you, I have never questioned your integrity. You need to stop expecting perfection from yourselves. I look at a man's heart Mac, and I have seen the goodness in you even though others have missed it at times. Now don't you think that if I can forget your errors and put them to bed that you should do just the same? In fact, if you can't forgive yourselves then you will never be able to recover that which was stolen from you that night. Grace and mercy are available for all who want it – some just don't quite know how to receive it – they take it but then go back to trying so hard to please me – the two don't work together – when you have the one, the other can't work. If you choose grace then live in it – with no guilt,' he added.

'Oh we want to live in grace. It sounds magnificent,' Mac said. This was all so new to them and would take them a while to unlearn some of their behaviours they had been so well schooled in. The Great One knew that but they would learn quickly – of that he had no doubt.

'Wonderful,' beamed Ziah. 'Receiving grace is that easy! Tell them what the rest of the plan is Father.'

He was like an excited child who couldn't wait for the surprise to be revealed.

'When you were attacked, that scroll you saw in the vision containing all the accusations against you was handed over to the Dark Lord. Cillian decided the Elders favoured you too much and wasn't sure that you would get the punishment he desired if he handed over the document to them, so he conspired to kill you instead and end your family's destiny by turning your children over to the dark side. If Sephtis should discover that you live, he will use it to cast spells that will hold you captive to those thoughts and make you feel unworthy and insignificant. If he can do that, you will never be able to rise from the ashes and be free again.'

'Who is Sephtis,' Imogene asked.

'Sephtis is the Dark Lord – that is his real name, although I believe he goes by the name Legion now.'

'He has a name?' Mac asked incredulous. Somehow they always just thought of him as an evil force, a being that had no identity but that of darkness.

'Everyone has a name Mac. Evil is something chosen and Sephtis chose to believe that he was everything his name implied. He became what he believed about himself. That is why it is so important for you to believe that you are able to conquer and that you are amazing. You are what you believe you are. Right now he is planning to use his magic and his evil followers to brainwash your children and to defile your memory and shame them. He knows it will erode their confidence and leave them susceptible to his rule.'

This horrified them both – it was bad enough that others thought poorly of them. They could cope with that, but the thought of their children believing those lies would kill them.

'What do we need to do?' Mac asked.

'You need to retrieve that scroll and destroy it once and for all. This will not be an easy task as Sephtis is devious and will do anything to keep your children captive to those accusations. Your one advantage will be the element of surprise, as he thinks you are dead.'

'How will we be able to win against the Dark Lord?' Mac whispered haltingly. He was feeling sick at the enormity of the challenge.

'I'm not sending you into this battle empty handed and alone. You will have weapons that I will give to you and you'll have some company with you. There is another member of my family that you will meet on your journey to

Sephtis. His name is Aedan – it means fire and he is not called that for nothing as you will see,' he chuckled.

'I want Imogene to stay here - to be protected and safe,' Mac stressed to the Great One.

'Unfortunately Mac, this is one battle you both need to fight but you will find that there is greater strength in your unity than you think,' he encouraged. Mac remembered those words spoken when the Great One had breathed life back into him.

'Come let's go and find the weapons you need to take with you,' Ziah cried in excited anticipation. Mac wished he felt half of Ziah's enthusiasm for the task ahead.

The Great One took them over to a chest that was filled with unusual treasures of all kinds. First he pulled out a pair of spectacles. These were no ordinary spectacles although to the average eye they looked just like any other pair. Putting them on, Mac discovered that he could see things in a completely different light. He could see through matter like walls and doors.

'Wow! This is incredible! It's like being in another world.' The irony of his comment was not lost on him – he was in another world here in Lionsgate.

'The warrior outside this door is taking a nap,' he said and they all chuckled together.

The next gift they received was a gold ring with a beautiful, unusual stone set in the middle.

'This is a truth ring,' said Ziah. 'You'll know when truth is being spoken or when lies are being told simply by looking at the colour of the stone. If it turns purple then truth has been spoken, but if it turns yellow you know that a lie has been told.'

The final gift they received was a small silver vial containing a special honey-coloured liquid.

'What is it?' Mac asked turning the jar over in his hands.

'This is very special oil with a beautiful fragrance. It comes from the Jasper flower here in Lionsgate and it has amazing healing properties. One dab can heal wounds or illnesses - it can even bring the dead back to life, but that would require the whole jar, so you need to be very wise what to use it for and when,' the Great One said.

Mac stored the gifts away carefully in a leather bag for their journey.

'These are unlike any weapons we've seen before,' Mac stated marvelling at the items.

'Yes,' Ziah replied, 'we don't fight battles with man's weapons – we do things differently here for the greater good of all.'

He was quite excited at being trusted with such special treasures and his earlier dread was evaporating as the treasures were revealed to them. He felt that stirring again – like when they had set out on their adventure to Griswold all those years ago. It was a combination of the unknown and the challenge that exhilarated him. This time however there was real danger involved.

'Use them wisely,' the Great One said, 'and keep them in your sight at all times. They would be a powerful weapon in the enemy's hand. I have one more thing to give you,' he informed them.

Gently he drew each of them aside and touched their heart with his hands. Power surged through his fingertips into the core of their hearts.

Removing his hands he said, 'you will respond differently now and be able to make decisions based on what your heart tells you and not just what your eyes experience. I have given you courage to perceive what is before you, hearts full of strength. Rest tonight for you journey on tomorrow. I look forward to seeing you both again soon,' he said affectionately.

Early the next morning, Mac, Imogene and Nuada set off to find Legion's domain.

They crossed the glass lake beside the huge city of Lionsgate in a boat pulled by three swans. The water shimmered, translucent and the ride was smooth and easy. The rest of the day they travelled through the countryside till they arrived on the outskirts of Griswold where they set up camp near a stream. It was strange being back in the land they had called home for so many years. They could feel the difference in the atmosphere from Lionsgate to this place. Looking at it now they could see how the ravages of the Dark Lord's reign had impacted on it. They sat around a warm fire eating their meal of cheese and bread with salted meat, chatting about what lay ahead of them and all the exciting things they had experienced in the Great One's presence.

Unbeknown to them, lurking in the shadows at the edge of the wood was something evil. He was Deception and he was determined to find the information the Dark Lord desired. He desperately wanted to win this challenge and receive recognition, although deep down he knew that it would be fleeting recognition as the Dark Lord was too self-absorbed to give credit to anyone else.

He had travelled throughout the kingdom and found nothing of interest. He had only heard people talking about the goodness of the Great One or acknowledging the Dark Lord's power, but nothing was that one juicy piece of information he needed. He was just about ready to give up when he chanced upon these travellers. Now, he sat craning his neck forward, his head cocked to one side so as to hear the conversation of these strangers. Every evil instinct told him that he would glean some information that would be useful to his Master. He was on the border of Griswold and this was his last hope before turning back for the castle.

'Yesterday was the most incredible day I have ever spent,' beamed Imogene. 'I can't believe there is so much life and love in the Great One's presence. I'll never forget it. Everyone should experience his love and goodness.'

'Yes,' Nuada said, 'he is one of a kind.'

Aislinn smiled at his description.

'How did you meet him Nuada? What is your story?' Imogene asked.

'I would not be here were it not for the Great One,' Nuada said. ''Thirty-two years ago I lived with my parents in the very castle we are going to visit.'

'What! You mean the Dark Lord's castle. THAT castle,' Mac emphasized.

'Yes, the Dark Lord wasn't always the legitimate ruler of Griswold. He had to usurp his power which he did by killing my parents. I was six years old when I saw them butchered in front of me. I was the rightful heir to Griswold when my parents died and he knew that. His men took me out into the deepest part of the forest and left me to die. I guess they hoped I would freeze to death, die of starvation or be eaten by wolves.'

'I am so sorry Nuada,' Imogene said gently touching his arm. 'It must be very painful for you re-living this nightmare.'

'He'll get what is coming to him – evil can only operate for a time before good people have a gut full of it and stamp it out.'

'So what happened in the forest?' Mac asked. 'How did you escape?'

'I was there for two days and had it been a moment longer I would have frozen to death or been eaten. I survived by climbing up into trees at night to sleep in the mossy branches. That was one thing the Dark Lord hadn't counted on. My father often took me out in the woods and taught me how to fight and take care of myself. He always said I wouldn't know when I would need it and that survival in our times was for the strong, the wise and the prepared. He never believed that having a position and title was enough to protect us and that proved true in his case. The Dark Lord managed to bribe some of our men and they opened the castle gates one night. My parents had no chance, but I was the lucky one. The Great One found me close to death and took me back to Lionsgate. He offered me a home and a place to belong and he taught me not to waste my life by being bitter and vengeful. You see, I understood more than you realized when I took you into that cave and showed you your past. I know how hard it is to forgive but also how important it is. I've walked in those shoes.'

'So the Great One has rescued many of us it seems,' Imogene smiled as she thought of how good he really was.

'Yes he truly is a remarkable man. He has been like a father to me and Ziah is like a brother. I have been most fortunate. I may have lost my inheritance but they have ensured that I have not lost my identity. You would understand that now after seeing Lionsgate.'

'Oh yes, it truly is a remarkable place. Meeting Ziah was the most exciting part of the day for me,' Mac said. 'I thought I really knew the Great One and yet all this time I never knew he had a son. He is full of surprise but somehow it makes him even more real and believable.'

'Yes, he's passionate about that boy.' Nuada said stretching himself out in front of the crackling fire.

'I can understand why.' Imogene was thinking of her own children and how she would do anything to see them safe again. She also thought about all that Nuada had lost and how he had turned into a remarkable young man. He was living proof that we decide who and what we want to become – that our destiny is decided by our choices and the roads we choose to walk. He was not trying to fight to win back his fortune and inheritance because he recognized that what he had in front of him – the people he cared for were more important than possessions and prestige. She admired him even more after hearing his story.

As they chattered over the events of the last few days, they were unaware of the delight of the evil eavesdropper in the trees. He could not believe his good fortune at hearing this news. Who would have thought that the Great One had a son? This certainly made him vulnerable, especially if he would do anything for that son. Deception knew he needed to make haste back to the castle with this tidbit of information before someone else got hold of it and shared it with the Dark Lord. He was equally surprised to hear how his Master had stolen Griswold from Nuada's family – he was more cruel and evil than he imagined, and Deception was glad he would be in the Masters good books – he would hate to ever be on his bad side.

'Tonight I have found a nugget of gold,' he chanted to himself. 'I'm going to be the Master's right hand man if I play my cards right.'

Mac, Imogene and Nuada were completely unaware their conversation would unfold events that would change history in Griswold forever. They had no idea of the battle that was to come and at what price it would come at.

They lay down contentedly next to the fire and each dreamed of the amazing experiences they had just had in Lionsgate and how their lives had been impacted by meeting him and Ziah. Their lives would never be the same again and a confidence was growing in Mac and Imogene that they would see their children again. One thing remained constant – they trusted the Great One implicitly.

⌘

Even though they were unaware of the events about to unfold as a result of their conversation, the Great One was completely aware of all that had transpired – he watched over them through his Mirror of Time and he saw the evil creature slink off into the darkness with this explosive new information. The Great One knew the consequences that would come.

## CHAPTER 8

# RANSOM

*You give but little when you give of your possessions. It is when you give of yourself that you truly give*

— Kahlil Gibran

AISLINN woke feeling refreshed and full of hope. She quickly washed her face and hands and tried to run her fingers through her wavy hair to detangle it. She peered out the barred window at the blue sky and whispered her thoughts to the Great One.

'Thank you for the wonderful gifts. It helps to know I'm not alone and that you know what we are going through.'

She gazed again at the beautiful gemstone Serena had given her – she could not believe that one stone could have so much beauty and worth. Just as they had promised, they had come each night when the young ones were asleep and watched over their innocent forms with tenderness and care. She had not yet shared her encounter with Struan and Maddy as she was unsure how to explain it. Part of her wanted to keep this experience close to her heart a little while longer as something unique and precious she had experienced. She feared sharing it would diminish it somehow.

The others began to stir for the day so she slipped her treasures back into the pillowslip. They were still quite sleepy as sleep was not easy with four of them sharing the rickety old bed.

'You kept kicking me in the night,' Struan complained to Maddy as he tried to stretch his stiff body.

'That was to stop you snoring,' she retorted. 'It sounded like a bear was sleeping in here.'

'Good morning,' Aislinn responded cheerily, trying to change the atmosphere of antagonism between the two. Before they could reply the key was turned in the lock. They all waited... uncertain and fearful.

The door swung open and the cloaked man stepped over the threshold. He set down a tray of food for the children and looked at them - a peculiar expression on his face. Aislinn couldn't quite work it out. Was it remorse or guilt she saw there, or was she imagining it? Whatever it was, she couldn't shake the nagging feeling that she knew him, but her memory would not reveal that answer to her. It was just a gut feel and it made her all the more uneasy.

⌘

The Great One watched the children tenderly. He saw the uncertainty written on Aislinn's face when she looked at Cillian – she was trying to process where she knew him from. She was a bright girl because even though he had chosen to conceal Cillian's identity from the children, she sensed somehow there was a connection between them. Their hearts would be crushed and their trust shattered for all time if they recognized him. He had been like an uncle to those children. For this reason they would not know his true identity when they looked upon him. What they were seeing was how Cillian looked with a dark side. All his jealousy and inner anger was being reflected and this is why he was unrecognizable to the children.

⌘

After breakfast, they were taken down to the kitchen. Aislinn was made to work doing laundry and Maddy helped cut and peel vegetables. Struan was put to work in the stables, cleaning and mucking out the horse stalls. Little Mitchell played at Aislinn's feet while she scrubbed and rinsed the Dark Lord's laundry. She punched his clothing as she washed and wringed them out, ridding herself of pent up frustration at being his prisoner, imagining she was punching his evil form. Still, it was good to be out of the tower room that was 'home' for now. The fresh air and space would do them all good even if they had to work and it would keep their minds off their parents for a short while.

⌘

In his chambers Legion perused the scroll that had been given to him by Cillian.

'What are your plans?' he asked.

'I'm going back to our village – I have managed to convince the Elders to make me the new leader of our clan in place of Mackenzie Hamilton.'

'So, you got what you wanted then – the allegiance of the spiritual leaders,' he said.

'I only managed to convince them after showing them that scroll. They would never have believed Mackenzie Hamilton was anything but perfect otherwise. They wanted to keep it but I told them that you had agreed to remove the problem of the Hamilton's in return for the scroll. They are too afraid of you to challenge it.'

'I always admire when hunger for something is rewarded – well my turn will be next. Your help has been very valuable to me Cillian.' He turned his attention back to the scroll dismissing him with a shrug.

'Close the door on your way out.'

Cillian left him to his reading – it was a long document and he had made sure every single mistake Mac and Imogene had ever made was written down in fine detail. He felt a measure of satisfaction – vengeance could be sweet. However he did still feel a measure of guilt when he looked at the Hamilton children – they had done him no wrong. The sooner he got away from here, the better. This place gave him the creeps.

Legion smiled as he read through the document.

'This certainly makes for interesting reading,' he mumbled. He was convinced his wizards and witches would be able to use some of it to cast spells that would keep the Hamilton children in bondage for a very long time. He carefully tucked it away in his treasure box and locked it with the set of keys he kept around his neck.

The commotion at his chamber door got his attention. Angrily he threw the door open with a bellow of annoyance at being interrupted. He was about to lash out at the perpetrator, but could not miss the victory reflected in his eyes.

'This had better be good,' he snapped. 'You've interrupted me.'

Deception crept forward silently but definite victory was engraved upon his ugly face.

'Yes Master, it is news of the best kind,' he gleefully said. 'I've found something extremely precious to the Great One.'

'Well what is it?' he snarled. 'Don't keep me in suspense, spit it out!'

'Before I do, I want your word that you will make me your chief advisor if this information proves valuable enough?'

Deception wanted assurance that he would receive his reward. He knew the lying nature of his Master.

'You know very well Drogus is my chief advisor,' Legion replied annoyed.

'Well then Master, I have to decide whether it is in my best interest to share this information with you. Perhaps someone else will find greater use for it.' he challenged.

'Silence, you impertinent fool! This information is obviously as precious as you say since you are overly confident in your demands. You will be given much influence if that is the case, I assure you, Now, tell me what you have discovered?'

'Did you know the Great One has a son?' he asked dramatically, waiting for his words to sink in. He enjoyed seeing his master at a loss for words, but even more the sense of power he felt momentarily.

Legion mulled over this piece of information. Of course the Great One would have an heir. It made complete sense if he wanted his kingdom to continue into the future. Still he felt shocked at this revelation and somehow even betrayed by it. He had not been good enough for the Great One even though he had tried everything to please him – he had been replaced by a son. Well that beloved son would be the old fool's downfall.

He smiled wickedly which turned into a wicked laugh and Deception knew he had hit the jackpot. He would be well rewarded.

'This is truly good work Deception. Welcome to life as an advisor in my court - this is priceless information indeed. All morning I've had fools at my door bringing me irrelevant, worthless information. At last something of value,' he smirked.'

This would be the beginning of the end of the Great One and his kingdom. He would make certain of that.

For now, Legion put aside thoughts of the scroll and using it to torment the Hamilton children. He had more pressing business to attend to. Rejection had been right - it was a brilliant plan. He would exchange the Hamilton children for the Great One's son. He knew the Great One would never allow the innocent Hamilton children to suffer and that he would sacrifice his son for the protection of the children. He could afford to give up the children if this would cripple the Great One. After all, once he was defeated Legion would control everyone, including those children. He called his scribes and had them write a ransom note.

*Four Hamilton children I hold in chains*

*Your only Son you must give away*

*His life for theirs will be the wager*

*Or else their lives are in mortal danger*

*Forty-eight hours to make the exchange*

*Or else they will all die in pain.*

Legion folded the letter, stamping it with his seal. He then called his fastest Monwing and sent him on his way with instructions not to return until he had delivered the message personally to the Great One.

As the monkey creature departed, Legion laughed.

'Tonight we will feast and celebrate for I feel that victory is close.'

News travelled fast around the castle that they would be celebrating a certain victory that night. Aislinn gleaned snippets of information as she worked down in the kitchen, and a feeling of unease grew inside her belly. For the Dark Lord to be so confident would mean that he was certain of beating the Great One and that could not be a good thing. She whispered her concerns to the Great One feeling alone and forlorn. As she ironed a large white feather fell in front of her and onto the garment she was pressing. She remembered what Ryder had said to her and how they would be protected while they were here.

'Thank you Ryder,' she whispered. 'I know you are here somewhere.'

# CHAPTER 9

# GRIEF

*I will not say, do not weep, for not all tears are an evil*

— J.R.R. Tolkien

THE MONWING flew as fast as his powerful wings could take him. He had no definite destination in mind as no one really knew where the Great One's kingdom was. He knew it was fortified against forces of darkness and evil and he had heard that to reach it one had to cross a glass sea. He flew out of the boundaries of Griswold, following Deception's directions to where he had seen the strangers who knew of the Great One's son, at their campfire. Of one thing he was certain - to fail to deliver this message would mean his death.

The Great One was aware of the message the winged creature was bringing as he knew and saw everything. He knew the creature needed to deliver the message, so he opened a gateway to his kingdom, allowing the Monwing to find his way to the Glass Sea.

As the monkey creature swooped over what looked like an ordinary lake a remarkable thing happened. The water that sparkled and glistened as the waves lapped transformed before his eyes into a very still and transparent sheet. It looked like glass and he could see his reflection in the lake as he flew overhead. The Monwing stared at his reflection, captivated by his looks - he had never seen himself in flight before and he quite admired what he saw. Finally it dawned on him that this was no ordinary lake. He did a circular swoop and shouted triumphant, realizing he had found the Glass Sea and his way to the Great One's kingdom.

In the distance he saw what looked like two huge wooden gates and pillars. He had never seen a village like this before – even the Dark Lord's castle paled in insignificance against this vast and beautiful architecture and yet it was not what he imagined the Great One would live in. He expected jewels, marble and vast wealth displayed. For a moment he doubted he had found the right place. At the entrance to the castle stood two, huge winged warriors waiting for his arrival. His admiration for his own winged strength quickly evaporated at the sight of these two – they were intimidating to say the least as they held swords that gleamed in the brilliant light and reflected in the beautiful sea.

He approached tentatively, only his fear of the Dark Lord keeping him moving. Their swords were raised to deter him from entering the gates. The winged creature was extremely curious about what was inside the gates and attempted to see past them.

'You may not enter these gates,' said the first warrior giant.

'I have a message to deliver to your master from the Dark Lord,' whined the Monwing, trying not to tremble. He felt dwarfed by their sheer magnitude.

'You may not enter this place,' said the second warrior more firmly.

'Goodness dwells in this place and if any evil tries to enter there are consequences. That unfortunately excludes you from entering Lionsgate'

'I need to make sure that he gets this message,' said the monkey uncertainly.

'He is expecting you and this message. You may leave it with us,' they replied.

The Monwing looked unsure. How did the Great One know he was coming? He was used to lies, deceit as everyone distrusted everyone in the Dark Lord's kingdom. He did not trust or believe these warriors.

'I really need to go in - I have strict instructions to personally deliver this message' he said with determination.

'All right,' said the first warrior, 'but don't say we didn't warn you.'

'What do you mean by that?' the Monwing sounded alarmed.

'Well, first your heart will be revealed as you enter Lionsgate – if there's no goodness in you, you'll instantly be changed into a statue of stone. We don't have a Monwing statue yet do we?' the one warrior asked the other.

'You mean I will die' the Monwing squeaked incredulously.

'That's about it' they said. 'Since you insist we'll open the gates for you now.'

'Wait, wait.' shouted the monkey in panic. 'That's okay, you can deliver the message – I'll wait here for the answer.' He didn't fancy becoming an ornamental statue even if this was the most beautiful place in the world.

He handed over the letter reluctantly and made himself comfortable at the gates to await a reply. He didn't see the wink the one warrior gave to the other as they made sport of him. Everyone was welcome in Lionsgate – no one was ever excluded, but they could not resist toying with the creature.

The Great One was ready and waiting for the message the warriors brought.

He tore open the seal and read the words, even though he knew what it said before he received it. He scanned the pages quickly, his brow furrowed, deep concern on his face.

Then he looked up at the warriors and said, 'Call Ziah please. I need to speak with him.'

Ziah bounded into the room with his usual exuberance and joy. The Great One's face lit up as he did – his affection for the young man clear. He was always in a good mood and nothing ever got him down. How he loved him!

'Father, you called for me?'

'Yes Ziah, I have something important to discuss with you.'

He told Ziah about the Hamilton children being kept as a ransom and how Sephtis wanted to exchange them for something from their kingdom.

'We must do it father. Nothing in this kingdom is worth more than their lives.'

'Yes Ziah, I see your heart. I too think they are worth fighting for and I love them dearly.' He stopped, emotion welling up.

'What is it Father? We can get what they want. We have enough wealth to spare?'

'No son,' he said earnestly, his heart breaking, 'he doesn't want jewels or gold. He wants you in return for the children. Somehow he has found out about you. I have tried to keep you from him because I know how evil he is and how he thinks, but now...' his words trailed off.

Ziah stared into his father's eyes and knew he was completely serious. He knew that his father loved him, but as the Great One he had no favourites – all were loved equally by him. He would not make him choose between them -it was up to him to make the decision.

'There's no choice. I love you father, and I love those children too. Their lives are of greater value than mine. They have their whole lives ahead of them. I could not live with myself if anything happened to them. I will take their place in Sephtis' castle. We will find a way to defeat him. We are stronger than his evil.'


Tears trickled down the Great One's face - he pulled his son toward him in a fierce embrace.

'I'm proud of you my son – you don't have to do this if you don't want to. It is your choice and I will honour it.'

'Yes I do– it is the only way to set them free. I will be all right. I have my keys.'

'We'll be together again soon my son. I love you no matter what.'

The terms of surrender were drafted for the Monwing to take back to Sephtis.

Ziah would be transported as far as the castle and then the Hamilton children would be exchanged for him at the gates. His life for theirs!

The Great One had no choice but to give Sephtis another opportunity to redeem himself. His word had meant nothing in the past and he only hoped that he would honour his promise to release the Hamilton children. If Sephtis chose to dishonour this agreement it would mean only one thing – war! His heart ached at the thought of losing his son – no one is ever immune to grief – not even the Great One himself.

CHAPTER 10

# LOYALTY

*Where the battle rages, there the loyalty of the soldier is proved*

— Martin Luther

MAC, Imogene and Nuada continued their journey toward the Dark Lord's kingdom, unaware of the turn of events. They were weary and their feet ached from the rough terrain. Their food supply was coming to an end and they desperately hoped for a small village with an inn to get a bath, a full belly and a good night's sleep. Their relief when they came upon the village of Trenton was tangible and they made their way to the nearest inn. Imogene looked forward to soaking in a hot tub and easing her sore muscles before catching some much needed sleep. Mac and Nuada were hoping for ale to quench their thirst and a good square meal. After settling in, they all sat in the pub area and ate a meal of thick vegetable soup with crusty bread and cheese. It was delicious and they ate till they could eat no more.

During their meal the inn progressively filled up with locals and travellers passing through Trenton. One man in particular caught Mac's attention. He had striking features and was quite unusual in appearance. He must have been well over six foot tall and strong with deep red hair and incredible green eyes. It was this combination that made him so noticeable. His emerald green eyes seemed to sparkle as if they were truly a jewel. His hair resembled flames of fire, but changed as the light danced upon it. He was not the kind of man who would pass unnoticed even though he sat quietly in the corner of the inn. His whole persona had presence.

Mac looked away, embarrassed that he had stared so much, feeling awkward that it might be perceived as rudeness. Nuada, noticing Mac's object of preoccupation, jumped up out of his chair and strode over toward the man. Mac panicked – surely he wasn't going to pick a fight. His alarm increased and he groaned inwardly at what was about to take place.

Nuada approached the man, standing over him like a bear, his hands on his hips. The stranger looked up lazily, his right brow lifted enquiringly and a bored expression on his face.

'Yes,' he said, 'can I help you sir?'

Nuada did not reply – he just stared the man down in a silent duel. The stranger stood to his feet and towered over Nuada yet still he did not back down. This was too much for Mac – he dropped his head into his hands – he was too old to be brawling in inns, but it looked like he might have to save Nuada. When he lifted his head the stranger and Nuada were hugging like long lost brothers. They slapped each other on the back laughing and joking with one another. Mac shook his head, relieved at the turn of events though he was still somewhat confused.

'It's been a long time, Nuada,' the stranger said. 'What have you been up to?'

'Oh just wandering to and fro like a lost gypsy, picking up some strays along the way,' he replied waving to the Hamilton's as he spoke.

'Come over and meet them.'

The stranger followed him over to Mac and Imogene's table and looked down at them with electric green eyes and a blaze of red hair.

'This is Aedan,' Nuada introduced. 'He's the other part of the Great One's gift to you on our journey.'

Mac and Imogene smiled, relieved that this big man with the wild countenance was on their side. They wouldn't want to be on the wrong side of him.

'So good to meet you at last. I've heard so much about you and have been following your journey with great interest.' He bowed low and kissed Imogene on the hand in a gallant gesture.

Mac and Imogene looked at one another in amusement. How on earth did this man know what was going on in their lives? Was the Great One connected to everyone?

Aedan pulled up a rickety old chair and sat down, his huge frame dwarfing the old chair.

'Another round of ale please,' he instructed the serving maid.

The inn was beginning to empty as men made their way home or off on a pretty young woman's arm. Only those who had passed out from too much liquor consumption or those staying at the inn remained and Imogene was glad for the less raucous atmosphere.

'So how do you fit into the Great One's family?' Mac asked with interest as they sat around the hearth enjoying the warmth of the licking flames. Nuada has told us his story. Did the Great One rescue you too?'

Both Nuada and Aedan let out peals of laughter simultaneously.

'No Mac, the Great One did not rescue me. It's quite difficult to explain, but we are a very tight team. We work really well together - each of us with our different strengths and personalities makes us a force to be reckoned with. I guess in some ways I have some very unique abilities that come in handy when people need help. I'm the person who visits your part of the world, helping people to find the Great One when they need to. I help those who are hurting and guide those who need guidance. You could say I am a jack of all trades.'

'Well we're delighted to meet you Aedan,' said Imogene. 'I feel as though I have known you forever.'

'Yes, people always tell me that. I guess that's why the Great One uses me to help people – they feel comfortable with me and in turn I help them through their troubles.'

'Don't let him sweet talk you Imogene,' Nuada teased. 'He can be quite a force to be reckoned with if you cross him. He's not all sugar and spice.'

Aedan playfully punched Nuada on the arm and the two shared a grin.

The four of them talked long into the night. Just being in Aedan's company refreshed them far more than sleep. Mac and Imogene were so grateful to the Great One for sending these amazing people across their path. Confidence kept growing within them to fight this battle.

As they settled into their comfortable bed that night, fresh after a good soaking in the tub and a full belly, hope stirred in them for the future. Things would work out fine. How could they not with these people fighting with them?

⌘

Mac woke to the sound of creaking floorboards. He lay as still as he could, listening to Imogene's even breathing next to him - tuning his ear for other unusual sounds. Something was not right - someone was in the room. The hair on his body prickled, a knot of apprehension gripped his stomach. He had experienced this exact feeling the night of the attack. The creaking came again, the intruder scouting the room for something. Mac opened one eye, trying to see who it could be, without alerting him to the fact that he had been discovered. In the corner of the room, in the dim light of the shadows, he spotted a small goblin with large, pointy ears and a big nose looking through his trouser pockets. When he found nothing there, he pulled at the leather bag containing the gifts the Great One had given them from over the back of the chair. He turned the bag over in his bony hands tugging at the cord, eager to see what was inside. He made little grunting noises as he tugged, his long, spindly fingers struggling with the knot. Mac's heart sank. They could not lose the glasses, ring and healing oil. They were vital for defeating the Dark Lord.

Mac lay still in the bed, mentally planning his surprise attack on the goblin. Suddenly, a gust of wind pushed open their door, rushing into the room like an angry tornado. *How was that possible?* It sucked and whistled, surrounding the goblin with such force, that the bag was ripped out of his hands as he spun like an out of control top. It was almost comical to watch. Mac sat wide-mouthed watching the spectacle, unsure what was happening before his eyes. It couldn't possibly be a tornado as the wind did not consume the whole room but rather moved as the goblin moved as though it were chasing the thieving creature around the room.

'Whoa...,' the goblin shrieked, terrified. 'Help me somebody. This thing is eating me alive.'

The wild wind teased and played with the frightened goblin before dropping him in an undignified manner on the floor at the door. The goblin did not wait for more – he scampered out the door as fast as his short little legs would carry him, shrieking in fear as he went.

By this time, Imogene had woken from all the commotion and she looked questioningly at Mac in her half alert state.

Mac, speechless in the bed simply muttered, 'Don't ask Imogene. I have no idea what just happened here!'

A hearty laugh erupted from the chair in the corner of the room leaving Mac and Imogene startled and a little afraid.

Aedan stretched in the chair as though this were an everyday occurrence for him.

'That should teach him a lesson he won't easily forget.'

'Aedan, how did you get in here?' Imogene asked incredulously, relieved to see him and not some other stranger in their room.

'I was keeping an eye on your room to ensure your safety, when that cheeky goblin snuck into your room to rob you. It's quite common – many travellers support these thieves quite well. I guess he thought you may have some interesting treasure. You really should keep these items from the Great One on you at all times Mac. If they should get into the wrong hands you could find yourselves in serious trouble.'

With that, he tossed the bag across the room to Mac who caught it and tucked it under his pillow.

'Lesson learned,' Mac said, relieved the items were still safe. 'What was that wind?'

'Oh that! It was me,' smiled Aedan. 'I'm not always what you'd expect as you will come to see in time. Now get some rest you two, we've a long day ahead of us tomorrow – and lock your door!'

He sauntered out the room leaving Mac and Imogene completely gob-smacked. Travelling with Aedan was clearly going to be an adventure and they sincerely hoped that he did not attract trouble wherever he went.

'I see what Nuada meant now – he's not all sugar and spice after all.'

They both laughed, grateful he had been around to chase off the thieving goblin.

'Time to get some sleep. We've got a big task ahead of us.'

# CHAPTER 11
# PRIDE

*A proud man is always looking down on things and people; and, of course, as long as you are looking down, you cannot see something that is above you*

— C.S. Lewis, Mere Christianity

THE MONWING arrived back at the Dark Lord's castle tired and cold. He did not have a good journey back from the Great One's kingdom - he got lost and had flown almost twice the distance. The Great One had helped him to find his way to his castle, because he needed the message delivered, but he was too preoccupied at what his son was about to do to worry about the creature and his flight plan home.

The monkey desperately wanted some refreshment, but he knew that he dare not even stop off for a minute to get something. The Dark Lord would be furious if he discovered that he had not made it a priority to deliver the reply to his message immediately.

He knocked at the Dark Lord's chamber and entered when ordered to.

'What news do you have?' he growled.

The creature immediately noticed the vast difference between the oppressive, dark room in this castle and the light, pleasant atmosphere around the home of the Great One.

'I have a reply from the Great One.'

'Let's see,' said Legion snatching the letter from the monkey. He tore at it savagely, desperation mixed with worry on his face.

'Yessss,' his shriek echoed through the castle in a piercing, victorious cry.

Everyone in the castle heard that cry. Something significant had happened.

Aislinn and her siblings heard it too, fear resonating through them like the gong of a drum.

Legion could not contain his malicious delight. He had outwitted the Great One himself and made him powerless. He dreamed of being the most powerful force in Griswold and beyond. What he would be able to accomplish with the Great One defeated was immense and beyond belief. This was the moment he had been waiting for, for many, many years. He had finally found the Great One's weakness – something he never ever thought was possible. So it seemed that the Great One had not taken long to replace him with a son but he would change all of that soon. He imagined the painful, slow death of The Great One's most treasured possession and how it would cripple his arch enemy forever. His life and pride were stolen when he had left Lionsgate– he should have been the rightful heir. Now he would steal the Great One's life and make it one of misery. Revenge would be sweet – even more so because it had taken a lifetime to get it.

⌘

Aislinn, Struan, Maddy and Mitchell sat in the tower, their courage beginning to waver. Maddy was tearful and missing her parents. She wished that they could all go home and wake up from the bad dream they were having. Struan continued to be angry and took out his frustration on the chipped stone of the tower wall by kicking at it continuously with his foot. Little Mitchell was unsettled - he was not used to being cooped up in a small space with nothing to play with. Aislinn felt she had let them down. All their resolutions to encourage one another and to keep their chins up had fallen by the wayside as each wrestled with their own frustration, pain and hopelessness. Their pride in their heritage had taken a knock – she did not want her brothers and sister forgetting who they were or where they had come from, yet this place seemed to steal hope. She knew the Dark Lord would love nothing more than for them to lose their identity and pride in their family name. It was up to her to keep that alive.

Aislinn had an idea. She would tell them a story using the characters she had met in the tower. Everybody loves a good story and hers would end by encouraging them all.

She called them over to the bed and they jumped up together.

'Once upon a time, there were four children who were captured by an evil giant.'

The children sat mesmerized as she wove the story of their capture and the three heroes who would come and save them.

'Ryder, Serena and Regent came riding in on white horses with an army of soldiers behind them to save the children,' she described dramatically.

They loved the story and the way that she told it, but the part they loved best of all was their daring escape with the three heroes. She finished the story, they all clapped in delight and she could see that they were encouraged again for a short while. She would have to find creative ways to distract them each day and to renew their faith in the Great One and their family name.

'How would you feel if Ryder, Regent and Serena were real and could save us?'

She felt it was time to tell them about the visitors sent by the Great One. She could not keep it to herself any longer – they needed hope and something to hold onto.

'Oh but they are real,' said Maddy matter of factly. 'I spoke to them last night when I couldn't sleep because of Struan's snoring. They'll help us I'm sure.'

Aislinn was delighted. So Maddy had met them too.

'Stupid dumb girls,' muttered Struan, 'they believe everything is real.'

Aislinn winked at Maddy and the girls smiled secretively.

⌘

Below in the castle dungeons, preparations were being made for the arrival of the Great One's son the following day. There was to be a strict guard over the dungeons as Legion did not want to risk being attacked by the Great One and having his son rescued. He had placed extra guards throughout the castle. He knew he could not wait too long for the trial to take place – it was too risky and he wanted nothing to prevent his victory.

There were others in the castle consumed with pride. Deception and Rejection strutted around issuing orders in loud, proud voices. Their promotion in the Dark Lord's ranks due to their part in making the plan a success. had clearly gone to their heads. They were certainly enjoying their new power, but it would be short lived as they would soon become hungry for greater power and recognition and the cycle of competition would begin again. In this kingdom there was no satisfaction, only a feeling of always wanting more.

⌘

The Great One watched all the events unfolding in Griswold in his mirror. He saw the Hamilton children and how they rallied together in a bad situation to stay positive and he felt a measure of pride in their strength. Then he saw how Sephtis preened and mentally congratulated himself on his success.

Pride is a funny thing. It can be both a positive and negative emotion. The Hamilton's were proud of their heritage and who they were and that was a good thing – it would stand them in good stead over the next few weeks and help them to overcome the challenges ahead. On the other hand Sephtis and his new advisors oozed a pride that was so putrid and would ultimately lead to their downfall.

'Yes Sephtis, your pride is self-seeking and greedy which makes you look inward. The Hamilton children's pride is based on gratitude to others which causes them to look outward. Your pride, Sephtis, will surely come before your fall.'

The Great One smiled – Sephtis was his own worst enemy.

## CHAPTER 12
# SURRENDER

*The greatness of the man's power is the measure of his surrender*
— William Booth

ZIAH steeled himself for the journey - he sailed across the Glass Sea with two companions as his father did not want him going alone. His mind was full with what was about to take place and even the clearness of the crystal sea could not bring him peace. Whenever he felt as though his courage might fail him, he thought of the Hamilton children and it gave him strength to go on, to see the task through. The situation they were in was not of their own making and he would do anything to see they were released. Once they reached land they met another companion, a Centaur, sent by the Dark Lord. He had a rough wagon to transport Ziah to the castle. The journey was slow and painstaking. Ziah was not chained as Legion wanted him to surrender of his own accord; it made him feel more powerful. He knew it was a risk as Ziah could escape at any time but he also knew the goodness of the Great One and that he would never leave those children to die. Knowing his enemy so well was very helpful.

Eventually the wagon ascended the crooked hill to the castle perched at the top. The sky was fierce and angry and the clouds rolled in furious billows around the tall turrets. The news of his arrival travelled fast in the castle.

'Move over, let me see over the wall,' some shouted as they pushed and shoved.

'Get out of my way, you're standing on my toes,' was a cry often heard as they tried to get a glimpse of the Great One's son.

Just like slime oozes through cracks, so each creature oozed into every available nook and cranny to see the arrival of the Great One's son.

Ziah was on trial and being judged except that he knew there would be no mercy or justice at this 'trial'. Slowly the gate creaked open and Legion himself stepped out to look at him.

'So you are the son of the Great One,' he said scornfully. 'You don't look like much to me. Tell me, what kind of Father would turn his son over to the enemy? It seems he doesn't love you as much as he should. I would have expected the Great One to give himself up long before throwing his son to the wolf.'

Ziah remained silent. He would not let this arrogant fool get to him.

Legion continued to mock and jeer Ziah. He wanted to humiliate the young man and to intimidate him. When he could not rattle Ziah he decided on another tactic.

'Strip him down to his under garments,' he ordered.

Instantly hundreds of little goblins all fell upon him ripping his clothing from his body as he was pushed and shoved between them.

'Give me that robe,' one Firegoblin screamed to another, pulling and tugging on his robe like a tug-of-war rope.

'It's mine! I had it first,' whined the other goblin pitifully.

While this was happening two others argued over his sash.

THE AWAKENING • 95

'Enough!' roared Legion. 'You goblins are annoying me and when that happens I am tempted to get the wizards out here to teach you a lesson or two. Now what's it to be?'

The goblins ears turned down, their shoulders slumped as they slunk away into the crowd of onlookers.

Legion turned back to Ziah, his eyes drawn to the set of keys dangling around his neck. Ziah had concealed them under his garments hoping they would not be discovered – this was going to be a problem, he needed those keys.

'What have we here?' he asked raising his eyebrows with interest. 'Remove those keys and bring them to me. Not only do I have the Great One's son, but it appears that I have some of his keys too. How interesting, we'll have to see what use they are to us. Perhaps these keys will unlock more of the Great One's kingdom,' he stated greedily.

Ziah sighed audibly. It was up to his father to rescue him now, for without the keys he would have a hard time saving himself from this evil lord.

'They won't be much use to you,' he said to Legion. 'They're not ordinary keys and only I have the authority to use them.'

'We'll see,' said the Dark Lord, another plan formulating in his mind.

'What about the Hamilton children?' Ziah asked 'I'm here in return for their freedom. You need to release them as you promised. I don't see them.'

Legion looked surprised at Ziah's challenge and then laughed mockingly. *How dare this young upstart make demands.*

'You don't seriously believe that my word would actually mean anything. I'm well known as the father of lies – it is not in my nature to be honest. It seems your father has forgotten who I really am. Those children have been a great help serving in my kitchen, so NO... I don't think I'll let them go after all!'

Legion was surprised at his own confidence and decision. He had fully intended to exchange Ziah for the children, but something about Ziah made him change his mind. His old insecurities and jealousies rose up afresh - the Great One didn't deserve anything in return. He would punish him fully.

'Take him to the dungeon!' he ordered impulsively.

'Going back on your word will wreak havoc on Griswold - my father will not tolerate your deceit, Sephtis' Ziah threatened as he was dragged away down the stairs to the dungeon waiting for him. There he was chained for extra security; his window barred and boarded so that no light could even enter the small, dirty little room. His only companions were cockroaches and a couple of rats. The son of the Great One was at the lowest place he could be, a prisoner, alone, and without his precious keys and worst of all, the Hamilton children were still not free.

⌘

Legion carried the keys up to his chamber thoughtfully.

'Get me Wizard Falstaff immediately,' he urged one of his messengers.

The messenger scampered off to find the wizard. Legion turned the keys over in his hands wondering what they were for. They were certainly unique.

He had been caught by surprise when Ziah called him by his old name - so the old man had told his son about Sephtis. It opened the old wound again. That name had to remain buried. If his followers found out about his history he would become the laughing stock of Griswold.

A knock at the door brought him from his musings as the wizard entered. He was old with a long white beard down to his belt. He looked questioningly at Legion.

'You sent for me Master.'

'Yes Falstaff. You are the wisest and most powerful wizard in my kingdom. Take these keys and see if you can work out what they are for and whether we can use them. They are from the Great One's kingdom. His son had them.'

'Certainly Master,' the old wizard replied extending his wrinkly old hand for the keys.

News spread rapidly through the castle - the Dark Lord was not releasing the Hamilton children after all and there was some speculation as to how the Great One would take that news. Some of the Dark Lord's subjects were casting lots and betting on what the outcome would be. Underlying everything was a feeling of fear in the ranks - these creatures knew that a battle of huge proportions could take place. The Great One would not take kindly to his deceit. He had overplayed his hand and was over-confident and they knew it, but they were too afraid to tell their Master for fear of joining Ziah in the dungeon.

Aislinn was taken from the tower and instructed to clean the Dark Lord's chambers. She felt terrified at the thought of being in his presence – she could sense his evil in every corner of the room as she entered. *Great One please protect me.*

'Come in child,' he tried to sound gentle and winsome. He had personally requested the young girl for the task. It was time she met him as his plan was to win her trust before he met the others. They would follow her lead then he would have all their allegiance.

She was not fooled by his sweet tone and she made sure not to look directly into his eyes. She hoped it would be perceived as submission rather than fear.

'How are you and your family doing?' he asked feigning concern. 'I trust you have been well cared for?'

'We are fine thank you Sir. We could use some more blankets to keep us warm if it's not too much trouble.' She was afraid to ask for anything, but her sibling's welfare gave her the courage to make the request.

'I shall see to it that some are sent up for you. It would not do to have you uncomfortable while you are my guests.'

Aislinn had to hold back a snort of disgust. *Guests, did he honestly think they were stupid enough to believe that especially since their door was locked?* She held her tongue.

'I need you to clean my chambers and put my books in order,' he instructed. 'Do you think you can manage that?'

'Certainly Sir, I will take great care of your books. I have a love for them and will treat them as my own.'

'In that case then, you may borrow one or two if you would like.'

'Thank you sir, I would like that.' Having something to read would be wonderful to pass the time when they were locked in the tower.

Legion was surprised at her compliance and beauty. She was indeed very pleasing to the eye and something stirred in his heart as she completed her chores. He resolved to win her over.

While she cleaned and polished and shelved books in his chamber she listened intently to what he was busy with, trying to glean as much information as she could. It could be useful for the future.

'Master,' boomed a voice in the doorway, 'I've looked at these keys and followed all the conversion spells I know, to no avail,' said Falstaff. 'They are unlike any keys I've ever seen. I shall have to seek out the druids to find out more about them,' he said.

'Those keys will not leave this castle,' Legion instructed. 'Go, if you must, but the keys stay with me. They are far too important to risk losing.'

Retrieving the keys from Falstaff, he opened his treasure box and placed them carefully inside. He did not notice Aislinn peering over his bent shoulder into the box nor did he see Ryder standing with his wings protectively open over her as she cleaned his chamber.

⌘

The Great One was furious at Sephtis' deceit. He had expected it, but he always gave an opportunity for redemption and was hoping that he would keep his side of the bargain. He discovered too, through the Mirror of Time, that the keys Ziah held were taken by him. The Great One knew that the keys would not be much use to Sephtis – he did not have the purity of heart to ever access them, but Ziah would have an impossible time freeing himself without those keys.

Trumpets blew throughout his castle as his followers all gathered to hear the news. One of their own was in trouble.

'We are fighting a battle. It's what Sephtis has chosen when he dishonoured the ransom agreement.'

'We're with you Great One,' a tall warrior stepped forward. Many more stepped forward following him. 'We'll get the chariots and horses ready.'

'Let's take back what is ours.'

Lionsgate was a flurry of activity as every warrior rallied together. Everyone loved Ziah – he was part of the backbone of Lionsgate and not one person feared what may become of them should they attack the Dark Lord's realm. Someone they loved was in trouble and that was enough for them to don their armour ready to fight the forces of evil. Sephtis had overplayed his hand by deceiving the Great One. His confidence had given him false hope and it was a decision he would surely regret.

# CHAPTER 13
# STRATEGY

*Give me six hours to chop down a tree and I will spend the first four sharpening the axe*

— Abraham Lincoln

'LOOK,' whispered Aedan to Mac and Imogene. 'At the top of that hill is the Dark Lord's castle. It's surrounded by a number of creatures that would love nothing more than to capture us. We have to be very careful and plan our way in,' he said.

Mac and Imogene had to keep their desperation for their children at arm's length. They could not let their feelings get in the way of making good decisions; otherwise they would all end up as prisoners of the Dark Lord.

'Let's settle down here, get some rest and clear our heads,' said Nuada, making himself comfortable on a grassy patch under a shady tree. In no time his eyes closed.

Thunk! An acorn hit him on the head.

'What the...,' he mumbled as another acorn hit him. 'Come out of that tree whoever you are before I shake you out,' he yelled.

A cheeky giggle emanated from the branches of the gnarly old oak tree.

'Is that you Morgan?' Aedan asked. 'What are you doing here?'

A young man dropped out of the tree, a broad smile on his face.

'I see you're resting again Nuada,' he said cheekily. Nuada responded by hitting him across the back of the head, but it wasn't a vicious smack, rather it was more affectionate and playful.

'I was one of the companions that accompanied Ziah to the Dark Lord's castle,' said Morgan in response to Aedan's question.

'What do you mean?' they all echoed in unison, confused. 'We were with Ziah just a few days ago.'

Morgan sat in the long grass with them and shared their lunch as he explained how Ziah had exchanged himself for the Hamilton children and how the Dark Lord had broken his agreement with the Great One by keeping them all as prisoners. Imogene was livid- she wished she had a moment alone with the Dark Lord.

*I would rip his heart out*, she thought protectively.

'This changes things,' said Aedan thoughtfully. 'The Great One won't take this lightly and is probably already preparing his army for battle. We must wait for them to arrive as we have a better chance of getting into the Dark Lord's castle with a whole army behind us.'

'Oh that's no problem,' Morgan chuckled, 'I know a secret way into the castle. I discovered it while waiting for the Hamilton children to be released to me. I overheard two of his men talking about the secret passage to each other, so I checked it out.'

'Where is it?' Nuada asked. 'It might be worth using the passage to scout out just what the Dark Lord is planning and how his castle is laid out. It could be a big help to the Great One's army when they arrive.'

Morgan explained how the passage went from the underside of the bridge, just outside the castle gate, under the castle wall to an underground well. At the well, it followed another passage to a flight of stone stairs that led up to the stables. The passage opened into a stall inside the stables. It was agreed that Morgan, Nuada and Mac would scout out the tunnel to see what they could discover.

⌘

Ziah sat in the dungeon – it was dark and unpleasant, but he was not worried about that. He chatted to his father, as he knew he could see him in the Mirror of Time.

'Father, I guess I messed things up a bit when I lost those keys, but I know that whatever happens, Sephtis will never win. There's too much at stake to lose this battle.'

As he spoke and shared his feelings and emotions, Ziah felt his father's love. That was one thing Sephtis could not steal from him. The dingy dungeon glowed as a magical light filled the room – the magic of love.

Ziah heard his words as the light shone so brightly in the room,

'I'm coming, son – take courage, this battle is going to be won.'

⌘

Aislinn took note of what the Dark Lord put into his treasure box. He was very protective of its contents which made her realize they were things of great value and importance to him. She noticed a large scroll in the box when he placed the set of keys inside. If only she could see more but he had tucked the key away in his pocket after locking the box. She thought about it as she sat in the tower room turning two books she had borrowed over in her hands.

'Aislinn,' a small, weak voice shook her from her reverie, 'I don't feel so good. My head hurts and I feel sick.'

Aislinn looked at Struan, surprised to see him pale and shivering with fever.

'Good gracious Struan, you look terrible,' she said, worry creeping into her voice. 'How long have you been feeling this way?'

He really did not look well so she quickly put him into the little bed and mopped his feverish brow as Maddy helped to place one of the new blankets they had received over him to quell his shivering.

'I think you have an infection in the wounds on your wrists. Try and get some sleep and I will see if I can get some healing ointment for you,' she said gently.

Maddy entertained Mitchell at the foot of the bed with the few stones they had found out in the courtyard earlier that day while Aislinn stroked Struan's brow.

⌘

Imogene sat with Aedan, in the protection of the thicket. It was dusk and the light was beginning to fade. She couldn't put her finger on it but she felt uneasy.

'Why are you so restless, Imogene?'

'I don't know,' she replied, 'I have a feeling that something is not right. I have a sense of worry for my children growing all the time and I can't shake it off.'

'You always were perceptive Imogene. That's why you have been used by the Great One to bring some clarity to people at times.' His voice was kind.

'You talk as though you know me so well.'

'But I do,' he said. 'I know everything about you because I'm part of the Great One's family and we know everything about the people we care about.

'How do you keep track of everyone?' Imogene marvelled.

'Let's just say that we have a magic mirror that enables us to see through time at everything each of you is going through. We also know exactly what you are going to do because of the talents and gifts we have given you - we know how you will use them. I'm part of the Great One's team that works here in your world. In fact I passed your home a number of times watching your family, but you would not have recognized me as I'm able to take on different forms when need be, as you have seen,' he chuckled remembering the inn at Trenton.

Imogene smiled too, remembering the times she had felt there was someone watching them and protecting them as a family. That must have been Aedan.

'Do you think everything will work out all right?' she asked, worry in her voice again.

'Everything works out well for those who believe in the Great One's goodness,' he said fondly to her.

⌘

'It's so dark down here,' Mac's whisper echoed through the stony passage.

'Yes, not the best place to be, that's for sure,' Nuada responded. 'How much further Morgan?'

'Not too far now, but we have to be very careful when we exit the passage so as not to be seen. We'll have to wait until nightfall.'

They waited a while till they were sure it must be night before Morgan carefully eased the passage door open an inch. He pressed his ear to the opening, listening for the sound of voices.

'Wait,' said Mac, 'I forgot I had these. We don't have to guess what's on the other side of this door. I have something that will help.'

He pulled the glasses out of the bag the Great One had given him and slipped them on. Instantly he was able to see through the door into the stable. He could see horses in their stalls and a stable hand sitting on the wall at the far end of the stable.

'What do you see?'

'We need to wait a few minutes until the stable hand goes for dinner. That'll be the best time to scout the castle as there will be fewer people around.'

They waited for what seemed like an age when eventually the dinner gong reverberated through the stony walls. The stable hand set aside his pitchfork, stretched lazily and headed out for his dinner. Slowly they pushed open the passage door and stepped out into the stable stall.

# CHAPTER 14
# CRUELTY

*Man is the cruelest animal.*

— Friedrich Nietzsche

BEFORE Legion headed to his banquet hall to feast on his success, he made a turn past the dungeon to see Ziah. He had reviewed his earlier plans and had a proposition to put to him - he could not wait to see how he would respond to it.

'I hope you are comfortable here,' he said sarcastically.

'I've stayed in better places,' Ziah replied, 'but I've also experienced worse than this,' he added bravely.

'Well, this doesn't have to be your lot.'

Ziah did not respond but waited for what was to come. He knew that Sephtis was planning something and he wanted to be prepared for it.

'I see great potential in you Ziah and I think we would make a formidable team. In fact I could offer you many things - wealth and power beyond your wildest dreams, and you wouldn't have to sit in the shadow of your father. You could be your own man, so to speak.'

'No thank you,' Ziah replied firmly. 'Nothing you could ever offer me is worth breaking my father's heart - as for wealth and power, I already have that as my father's heir. I don't need your pitiful offer.'

'Now that is where you are wrong...' the Dark Lord spat in anger and frustration.

'I've been in your shoes before Ziah. You see, I was once like a son to your father. Did he ever tell you that?'

He saw the shocked look on Ziah's face.

'No matter how hard I tried to please him it was never good enough. That is when I realized that I could be whoever I chose to be. I was tired of being poor, weak Sephtis and I chose to become Legion – a leader and ruler in my own right – not somebody else's side-kick. You can come out from your father's shadow if you align yourself with me.'

'I'm not surprised that you could not earn my Father's love. You obviously didn't know him very well even though you claim you were like a son to him. You see, no one can earn his love because he loves unconditionally – it doesn't require effort on your part at all. It was your greed and insecurity Sephtis that made you who you are today. I don't live in my father's shadow but rather I live in his love.'

'Don't ever call me Sephtis again Ziah – my name is Legion. You're a prisoner here if you hadn't noticed! There will be no inheritance for you and I certainly don't see your father breaking down the doors to rescue you, do you? This is a one-time offer Ziah.'

'You're right,' Ziah said calmly, 'but he'll be here, and you will wish you had never begun this war. You can call yourself by whatever name you choose but a name doesn't make you who you are – it's the heart that makes the man and yours has not changed despite your name change.'

Legion slapped him across the cheek with all the force he could muster. Ziah was momentarily knocked backward, but he stood upright with pride and courage, his face set in determination.

'Guards, perhaps our little friend needs some persuasion as to how bad things could become for him here. Teach him a lesson, but don't kill him – that will be MY pleasure!'

With that he stormed off to have his dinner.

⌘

Mac, Nuada and Morgan crept around the castle like mice out looking for scraps of food, wary they might bump into the big, bad cat at any moment. Mac wore the glasses as it enabled him to see what was around each corner or behind each door. They decided to find the dungeon in the hope of seeing Ziah and the Hamilton children. They crept down the stairs toward the dungeon of this evil castle where they heard taunting, mocking voices.

'So you think you're better than us and above us, do you?' shrieked a high-pitched voice. This was followed by the sound of a whip being cracked and hitting a soft flesh target.

'Aaarghh...' A grunt of pain followed.

The three crept as quietly as they could behind the stair wall and hid in the shadowy recess. They watched in horror as Firegoblins attacked and beat Ziah. They kicked him and spat on him. One particularly evil little creature tried to poke his eyes out with his long spindly fingers, and they took turns pulling at his hair till handfuls came loose.

They watched, tears' rolling down their cheeks as the Great One's son was beaten to within an inch of his life - they felt helpless as they could do nothing to help him.

They were not the only ones weeping! The Great One could see in his mirror what Sephtis was doing to his son and his heart broke. He turned away from the mirror as it was too agonizing for him to watch and comprehend.

'My boy, my boy! What are they doing to you? Hold on, it won't be forever.'

'Excuse me Great One,' echoed a voice from the doorway. 'The army is ready and waiting for your command to move out.'

'Let's go,' he said.

⌘

Mac, Nuada and Morgan arrived back at the thicket silent and sober.

Imogene was full of questions, 'did you see the children, what happened....?' On and on she threw questions at them.

Mac eventually drew her aside cautioning her to stop.

They described what they had seen in the dungeon and Aedan glowed with fury, pain, love and compassion for Ziah. He certainly was born of fire as his name implied. Fire is always hottest and most dangerous when it burns with a white flame and something ignited within Aedan, which made him a dangerous man. That was his brother they beat so cruelly.

He drew himself aside to talk to the Great One.

'Come to us quickly Great One,' he urged in groans of pain. 'Ziah needs you, he's in trouble -I fear that the Dark Lord is going to kill him.'

Imogene felt the same unease she had felt earlier creep back into her heart. The Dark Lord was more evil than she imagined and she worried about her children. Were they all right? Were they even alive? Mac had said that they hadn't seen them in the dungeon.

'What if the Dark Lord has killed them, Mac?' she cried. 'Perhaps that is why he never exchanged them for Ziah, they must be dead.'

Her mind raced and filled with crazy pictures and scenarios.

'Don't fret, Imogene,' he chided. 'The Dark Lord does not play by the rules or fairly. The fact that he never exchanged them with Ziah does not mean they are dead. We have to keep our faith up. The Great One wouldn't send us to get them back if they were dead – he knows everything.'

'I just want them back and for this nightmare to end,' she said forlornly. 'I want things back the way they were.'

'Imogene, things will never be the way they were,' Mac responded with a mixture of gentleness tinged with frustration.

'We can't turn back the clock. Would you even want to go back to the way things were now that we know what we know? We are different now, we think differently. What was once our mission is no more. We have a new future. When we get what was stolen from us, things will look brighter,' he promised kissing her on the forehead.

# Chapter 15

# Distress

*If you are distressed by anything external, the pain is not due to the thing itself, but to your estimate of it; and this you have the power to revoke at any moment*

— Marcus Aurelius, Meditations

STRUAN moaned in feverish sleep as his temperature soared and infection ravaged his young body.

'Help somebody... help.' Aislinn beat the tower door with her fists. She was becoming hoarse from all the shouting and Mitchell and Maddy whimpered at the end of the bed. They had not seen her show fear in all the time they had been away from their parents, and her desperation frightened them.

'Aislinn,' whispered a gentle voice from behind her as she stood at the door.

'Ryder!' she exclaimed relieved, 'thank goodness you're here. Please do something – Struan is so ill and nobody will help us. Can you heal him?' she asked hopefully.

'No I am not able to heal him. We're only here to protect you - that is all.'

He smiled at Maddy and Mitchell who stared at this stranger with big baby eyes. 'Every battle has to be won by you, including this one, but I will cause a distraction outside your door to attract some attention up here, then maybe he can get some help.'

'Thank you Ryder, I don't know what else to do.' She rinsed the cloth and bathed Struan's face with the little water she had left in the basin.

'Try and keep his fever down as much as you can, Aislinn,' Ryder said as he disappeared straight through the wall before her eyes.

A few minutes later she heard a commotion outside the tower door. Whatever Ryder had done, it had been effective as a key turned in the lock and opened their door.

'What's the problem in here?' a gruff old man asked Aislinn. 'You children are making a nuisance of yourselves and distracting us old people from sleep on the next floor.'

'Please sir,' Aislinn mustered as much courage as she could, 'my brother has a bad infection and a high fever. He needs medicine or he may die,' she begged.

'And what makes you think that I would care.' It was said cruelly. 'It would be one less noisy child to deal with each day.'

'Please sir,' she continued to plead, 'the Dark Lord would be angry if he had plans for us and they were ruined because we were not cared for. Who would help do his laundry and muck out the stables for him?'

Manipulation would be the method to get what she needed. She had observed how everyone in this castle was terrified of the Dark Lord and she knew this was her best shot at getting help. This was her only chance.

At the mention of the Dark Lord's name, the old man's demeanour changed.

'I'll see what I can do about getting some salve for the infection, but that's all I can do. In the meantime, keep the noise down in here' he grumbled as he exited the room.

⌘

Deep below in the dungeon was another in pain. Ziah lay on the hard, cold stone floor, his body bruised and aching in every way. He had crushed ribs and was covered in welts from the whipping he had received. He could barely move; the pain so severe each time he tried to change position.

'Father, father, please be with me,' he cried, but there was silence in response. He felt alone, small in this overwhelming, evil place. *Where was his father?*

⌘

Heading across the plains of Griswold, a thunderous noise of thousands of horses' hooves as the Great One's army stormed the plains in urgent strides. Leading the procession was the Great One himself, riding Pegasus, his winged, white horse. They were racing against time and the urgency of their mission changed the landscape from peaceful flowing hills to a moving mass of warriors. To the onlooker it appeared as though a dangerous and powerful storm was about to unleash itself upon the Dark Lord's territory.

⌘

Aislinn heard the approach of footsteps outside the tower door. She breathed a sigh of relief. It had been a while since the old man had left and she was afraid he had gone back to bed ignoring their plight. The key turned in the lock, revealing a woman behind the disgruntled old man. The wrinkled old woman entered the room with a jar of ointment in her hand and some bandages. The old man carried a pitcher of fresh water.

'Let's see what we can do for the young man,' she said in a wavering voice. Her face looked worn and creased as though she had worked hard all her life but Aislinn could see that she had once been a beautiful woman. Is this what living here did to one?

Slowly she bathed Struan's wounds and rubbed salve on his cuts before binding them with fresh bandages all the while soothing him in a motherly voice. Aislinn mopped his feverish brow and he mumbled incoherently as he fought the fever. Thankfully Maddy and Mitchell had fallen into an exhausted sleep.

'His fever looks very bad, young one. I'm not sure whether he will make it through the night, but if he does, he will have a chance of surviving.'

Aislinn could see a measure of compassion in the woman's eyes, but as fast as she saw it, it was covered over with a glazed expression. Emotion was not encouraged in Griswold –it was for the weak.

Her heart sank at this news and for the first time she felt totally alone and helpless. The old couple stood up and left the room, locking the door behind them as they went. Aislinn felt spent and sank to her knees on the floor, her tears wetting the edge of the bed as they flowed freely down her face.

'Help us Great One,' she begged. 'Please, don't leave us now!'

'They're coming to get me..... help me please,' Struan mumbled in his delirious sleep. He tossed and turned and beat the air as feverish dreams filled his mind with all sorts of evil. Aislinn continued to cool his brow as she watched over his weak body. She felt helpless. *I'm sorry Mama, Papa. I have not protected them.*

⌘

Imogene tossed and turned on her bracken bed under the stars. She could not let go of the feeling that her children were in danger and that something was wrong.

'Please protect them and keep them safe,' she whispered.

Legion also tossed and turned in his chamber. Sleep eluded him - he was troubled by Ziah's confidence at being rescued. The night watch had been trebled to make certain no attack would take place while they were sleeping. He could feel the taste of victory in his mouth, but he still had a sense of unease in his gut. He would need to convince Ziah to join him – he needed him more than he wished to admit. A son turning against his father would be even more painful than his death. Dying for the Hamilton children would be a noble thing to do in his father's eyes, however, betraying him would crush the old fool. Still, if Ziah could not be turned he would have to kill him. Time was of the essence and he could not take too long to persuade the young man. With a sigh he turned over again and tried to get some sleep.

# CHAPTER 16
## STOLEN

*Ordinary riches can be stolen; real riches cannot. In your soul are infinitely precious things that cannot be taken from you.*

— Oscar Wilde

THE SUN rose, the sky exploding in beautiful orange and pink streaks. The Great One's army settled into the valley just below the Dark Lord's castle. They blended into the shadows to remain concealed - the element of surprise vital. There they would remain for the day and plan their attack carefully for nightfall.

Imogene and Mac awoke to the smell of coffee brewing on the fire. Aedan smiled at them as they stretched and rubbed the sleep from their eyes. Imogene looked exhausted and Aedan handed her a mug of coffee - he was aware of her restless sleep the previous night.

'Today will be a day like none other. Things are going to happen that will change our history and we need to keep our energy and strength up.'

'What do you mean, Aedan?' Mac asked nervously. 'What do you know?'

'I've been in contact with the Great One. His army is camped in the next valley below the castle. We will meet with them later today and we'll show them where the secret tunnel is. When nightfall comes, we are going in.'

'Finally, we get to take back what is ours,' Mac sighed.

⌘

It was a difficult night for Ziah. His body and muscles ached and resisted movement. He groaned inwardly and his head throbbed as though a million daggers pierced his brain. The lashes on his bare back had dried in caked blood and as he moved they began to seep again. His body and heart felt bruised. The magnitude of Sephtis' evil and hatred was evident to him - he knew death was a real possibility. His frustration at not being able to help the Hamilton children kept him going. He would do whatever he could to secure their freedom. He recalled his conversation with Sephtis the previous night. He would never sell himself. Nothing would lower him to that level. Besides, Sephtis had proved he was not trustworthy when it came to making deals.

'I know you're on your way Father,' he whispered to himself. 'You would never leave me at the mercy of this evil.'

As he spoke his heart lifted a little – his body may be battered, but his spirit would not give in.

⌘

Legion woke feeling positive. He had made a decision during the night. He would approach Ziah once more before breakfast and offer him a chance to change his allegiance. If he should refuse, then he would make sure that by the end of the day he would be breathing no more. He took great pleasure in thinking how he would first torture Ziah before the final, fatal blow.

'Today is the day I finally reach the pinnacle of my success. Either Ziah will join me, which would be first prize, or he will die – whichever way it goes things can only get better from now on.'

He strutted around his chamber arrogantly allowing himself to dream of the power he so desperately desired.

He rang the bell for his valet to come and ready him for breakfast.

'Get my clothes and have the wizards join me for breakfast,' he snapped at the little goblin dutifully assembling his attire.

The goblin scuttled off to notify the wizards of the Dark Lord's request, leaving him to dress and preen before his mirror.

As soon as he was ready, he made his way down to the dungeon to offer Ziah his final opportunity to become an ally of Griswold.

He descended the stairs, convinced that Ziah would have changed his mind after the brutal beating he had received.

'Surely no man is stupid or brave enough to endure further unnecessary torture,' he muttered to himself. 'The offer of a better future will surely sway him now.'

He expected to find the beaten Ziah crumpled in a heap, defeated and alone as he approached the dungeon. He was to be disappointed.

'What's that noise?' he asked the guard trying to tune his ear to the unusual sound he could hear coming from within the cell.

'It's the prisoner, my lord. He has been singing since early this morning and it has increased in the last hour.'

Legion looked incredulous. *Singing?* Was the man mad? This was followed by a fury that erupted deep within his soul. His face turned crimson, a sneer of disdain appearing across it.

'Is he trying to mock me? I will have the last laugh yet. Open this door,' he commanded.

The door swung open to reveal Ziah's bruised form, but instead of defeat he appeared confident and defiant to the Dark Lord.

'Good morning,' Ziah said jovially. 'I hope you slept as well as I did?'

'So you want to play that little game do you?' replied Legion sarcastically.

'I trust you have thought about my proposition overnight and are ready to reconsider?'

'I thought I had made myself rather clear last night that you would be the last person on this earth that I would ever align myself with. Nothing has changed since then other than the fact that you have tried to beat me into submission. Thank you for strengthening my resolve.'

He watched, Legion's face, a frozen mask as the insult sank in.

'Suit yourself then, you have just signed your own death warrant. I hope it was worth it? Enjoy your breakfast Ziah - it will be the last you ever have!'

⌘

Aislinn was relieved to see Struan looking a little better in the morning. He seemed more peaceful and rested. She fed Mitchell his breakfast while picking at her own. She wished she could get Struan to eat something as it would strengthen him, but at the same time she didn't want to wake him as he needed the rest. Her thoughts were interrupted as the tower door swung open and the old woman who had helped her the night before came into the room.

'How's he doing?' she asked glancing at Struan.

'He seems much better, thank you,' Aislinn replied.

'I've come to take the little one,' the woman said quickly, noting the alarm in Aislinn's eyes.

'Wha... what do mean?' Aislinn stammered unsure she had heard correctly. 'Where are you taking him? You can't take him. He's just little. He needs me.'

'I'm sorry lass. It's the Dark Lord's decision – he has decided there is no use for him here and that he hinders your work. He is giving the little one to one of the wizards and his wife. They have been trying to have a child for years, but not even his magic has been able to produce an heir for them,' she explained looking down at the floor, unable to look Aislinn in the eye.

'No...'she wailed. 'You can't take him. He's not a possession.'

She jumped up reaching out for the little boy. Before she could reach him he was scooped up by the guard accompanying the woman. Helplessly she watched as the crying little boy was carried out the door.

'Linnie...' he wailed using his pronunciation of her name -it broke her heart to hear it.

Would they ever see him again?

Maddy sat hunched in the corner, her shoulders shaking as she wept uncontrollably.

'W...w...will they take me away Aislinn?' she asked. 'Please don't let them take me, I'll work hard,' she pleaded. All Aislinn could do was wrap her in her arms and comfort her. The Dark Lord did not realize that he had undone all his 'kindness' by taking Mitchell Hamilton. Aislinn despised him now more than ever.

⌘

The Great One's army readied themselves for battle, determined to get Ziah and the Hamilton children back safely. They prepared their weapons and planned their attack carefully. They would wait until dark and then use the secret tunnel to breach the castle. Some of the warriors would creep up onto the battlements and quietly silence the lookout guards. Others would head for the dungeon and release Ziah. They knew that the children were not in the dungeon as Aedan had passed this information on to them, so another team of warriors would look for them.

'Where do you think they could be?' Morgan asked.

'We know,' resonated a voice that was familiar but had not been heard for a while.

'Ryder! It's good to see you again – how are you?' Morgan asked embracing his friend.

'We are well, and glad you are here. This place is so evil and those children need you,' Ryder said seriously. 'They are being held captive in the tower room on the south side of the castle.'

'That is good news to hear,' Morgan said. 'The more we know the easier it will be to put our plan into action without drawing too much attention to ourselves,' he said.

'Let's go and meet Aedan and the Hamilton's. We need to make sure everyone knows exactly what they have to do tonight.'

⌘

Legion was still very angry as he sat at breakfast. How dare that impertinent young man turn down his offer! It fuelled his fury just thinking about it. His wizards were talking animatedly amongst themselves and his youngest wizard Morelock was especially excited and gracious as he had been granted the request of a child in the form of Mitchell Hamilton. His wife had seen the little boy playing in the kitchen while Aislinn had worked and his beautiful blond curls and angelic face had won her heart. It was a sore point for Morelock that they were unable to have a child of their own. He felt useless as a wizard as this was one wish he could not perform or grant. He had no spell for creating life and his wife's nagging and tears were beginning to wear him down, so much so that he had been tempted to turn her into a frog. Fortunately for her it was only a fleeting thought. This was a new beginning for them both. He had dreamed of a son to teach all his wizardry skills to.

'Summon my heralds,' Legion ordered. Instantly there was scurrying of goblin feet as they hurried off to call for the heralds. This usually meant the Dark Lord had an important announcement to make.

'You called Master.' They entered the banquet hall.

'Yes, I want you to notify everyone in Griswold that at the ninth hour today there will be a public execution of a traitor to my kingdom. Everyone is welcome and there will be a feast provided for all who attend afterwards.'

'Yes Master,' they answered preparing themselves to head out into all of Griswold with this news. Griswold wasn't particularly big and the news would travel fast, but people required time to travel to the castle and the Dark

Lord wanted as many of his subjects to witness the demise of the Great One's power.

'Dispatch this news quickly to the furthest parts of my kingdom by the Monwings,' he said.

Legion knew the promise of a feast in his castle would draw in many people from Griswold who were not only curious, but who also wanted a sumptuous meal and an endless supply of fine wine and ale. The villagers would come in their droves.

Ziah must feel humiliated in front of an audience. He would be cut down to size.

'It's all coming together, at last,' he said gleefully.

⌘

Aislinn was still trying to come to terms with Mitchell's absence. She felt as though another piece of her heart had been ripped out and she wondered how much was left of it. If another piece were to be stolen, she felt sure she would die.

The key turned in the lock attracting her attention and instantly Maddy cowered under the rickety bed, convinced she was next to be taken.

'Come with me,' the guard said to Aislinn. 'The Dark Lord has a big feast happening tonight and he needs all the help he can get preparing for it.'

Aislinn stood to her feet, worry etched into her face as she glanced over at Struan who still lay weak upon the bed.

'My brother is very ill - who will take care of him?'

'That is none of my concern,' he replied impatiently. 'You need to come too,' he said waving at Maddy. 'Hurry up we don't have all day.'

The girls followed him down the tower stairs to the kitchen they were so familiar with. They could hear the kitchen staff talking about the execution that was going to take place that day, and Aislinn felt her blood run cold. Who were they going to execute?

'It's someone very important,' she heard the head cook say to one of the kitchen hands.

'Apparently, he's a traitor in the Dark Lord's kingdom and we all know what that means. He's likely to be tortured on the rack first.'

'I heard he turned down great riches and power the Dark Lord offered him,' one young kitchen maid said.

'Don't believe everything you hear, silly girl,' the cook chided. 'No one would be stupid enough to turn down the Dark Lord.'

They became aware of Aislinn, staring open mouthed at their conversation and the cook chased her off to help with polishing the silverware.

She was most curious. Who was this mystery person to be executed? Clearly it was someone who recognized the Dark Lord's complete evil and wanted no part of it. You had to admire him for that. She had heard rumours around the castle they were to be exchanged for the Great One's son, but she wasn't sure about that, as no one had said anything to them. As far as she knew, that was just a tale. She had never heard that the Great One had a son – certainly her father had never mentioned it to her. She really hoped it wasn't his son that was going to be executed – that would be terrible.

Before long she completed her polishing. It seemed like a quick task as her mind was preoccupied with Struan, the execution and Mitchell. She hoped Struan was okay. It worried her that she was not there to monitor his fever.

'The Master has called for tea in his chamber,' the head cook said. 'Make up a tray for him and take it up,' she said to Aislinn. 'We're too busy here to stop our preparations.'

⌘

Aedan, Imogene, Mac and Nuada were all listening intently to Morgan's plans for the attack. They had joined up at last and were running through the strategy for that evening. They sat around in the shade of a tree, posing as travellers passing through the countryside. Hidden in the nearby forest, concealed to the naked eye was the entire Great One's army ready to move at nightfall.

'I'm feeling a little nervous,' Imogene said, 'but I can't wait to see my children again and see the Dark Lord defeated once and for all.'

'Hear, hear,' said Aedan. 'That is something we all look forward to and by tomorrow we will be celebrating their return.'

The sound of an approaching horseman reached their ears.

'Quiet,' Aedan said. 'Remember we are just passing through Griswold. Imogene and Mac, hide your faces in case you are recognized.'

Imogene quickly pulled her cape hood over her head and Mac pulled his cap down low over his eyes. It would not do to be recognized now.

The horseman approached and they recognized him as an official herald from the Dark Lord's castle by his attire.

'Good morning,' the herald said. 'Are you on your way to the castle for the execution today?'

Aedan tried to keep his tone neutral and nonchalant.

'No Sir, we are just passing through Griswold. We know of no execution'

'Well if you are looking for a good meal then attending the execution will ensure you feast well tonight. It may be worth your while to delay your travel through Griswold till tomorrow.'

'Who is being executed?' Nuada asked feigning curiosity.

'He is a traitor to the Lord of Griswold. The execution takes place at the ninth hour. You would be most welcome. '

'Thank you,' said Aedan politely, trying his hardest not to let his anguish show. He knew the 'traitor' was Ziah and his heart was pierced to the core.

The herald clicked his heels and his horse moved off down the path to pass on the grim news to others in Griswold.

'What are we going to do?' Morgan was incredulous at this new piece of information.

'If we go in tonight it will be too late to save Ziah, but if we go in during daylight we will risk many more lives. What should we do?' Nuada asked.

He knew how close Aedan was to Ziah and could see the look of pain on his face. He felt it too, as Ziah was like a brother to him. He had to consciously push down the resentment and bitterness he had pushed down all the years ago toward the Dark Lord. He would not become like that man! He had worked too hard to choose goodness in his life.

They all looked to Aedan for the answer. This was a twist of events that none of them had anticipated.

'I will seek the Great One's advice.' Aedan strode off into the forest to speak with the Great One and get his counsel.

The rest of the group said nothing - each of them plagued with their own thoughts and imaginations.

⌘

Aislinn tried to still her shaking hands and nerves. It would take all her strength not to vent her rage at the Dark Lord. Oh how she hated him, yet she feared him all the more He was the personification of evil. She looked at the tea tray and wished she had a vial of poison to throw into the pot. She thought again of little Mitchell and wondered if he would be all right. She sent a mental prayer to the Great One as a lone tear trickled out her left eye. She brushed it away angrily – now was not the time to let her emotions overwhelm her.

He was the reason her family had been torn apart – he had killed her parents and taken her baby brother and now she was to do his bidding while her other brother lay desperately ill and alone. If anything happened to Struan she vowed she would personally kill him.

'Hurry lass, the Master won't wait forever for that tea and Cook will have your head if he takes it out on her.'

'Aislinn scooped up the tray, her hands still shaking; this time from rage as she exited the kitchen.

## CHAPTER 17
# DISCOVERY

*It is by going down into the abyss that we recover the treasures of life Where you stumble, there lies your treasure*

— Joseph Campbell

AISLINN carried the tea tray up the stairs to the Dark Lord's chamber. She always dreaded coming in here, a knot of fear twisting her stomach. As she walked down the corridor to his chamber she heard a whisper calling her name from a side niche.

'Aislinn... Aislinn!' the voice called urgently.

She looked around unsure where the voice had emanated from.

'In here,' the voice echoed off the stony facade.

She slipped into the niche and came face to face with Regent.

'Regent!' she squealed in delight almost spilling the tea. 'What are you doing here?'

'We have an important task ahead of us Aislinn and we need your help,' he said.

'I'll do anything to help you,' she replied eagerly.

'It will be very dangerous for you,' he cautioned, 'but....'

He was silenced by her.

'Nothing will prevent me helping you to overcome the Dark Lord,' she whispered fiercely. 'He has stolen every precious thing from me. I want justice!'

He knew she was serious as her eyes flashed in anger and the glimpse of pain he saw there made him catch his breath.

'So be it,' he said. 'They are going to execute the Great One's son today at the ninth hour and we need to get hold of the set of keys they took from him when he arrived here. They are very distinct keys, shiny gold and unlike any other keys you will see.'

She gasped. 'I know those keys. I have seen them. The Dark Lord was very curious about them and has locked them safely away in his treasure box.'

'Do you think you could get them?' Regent asked.

'He keeps the key for the treasure box around his neck and never lets it out of his sight.' She was dismayed.

'We'll think of something,' Regent encouraged. 'You had better get him his tea before he gets suspicious. Keep your ears open for any information you might hear in his chamber. I'll talk to you later.'

With that he was gone. Aislinn picked up the tray and hurried down the corridor to the chamber.

'About time,' Legion shouted as she entered the chamber. 'I was beginning to think you were harvesting tea leaves it was taking so long.'

His sarcasm was not lost on her and she apologized politely for the delay. She did not want to anger him - she needed to be in the chamber to see what information she could gather. She had to put aside any feelings of loathing she had for him, and focus on her task. I must not think of

Mitchell now, or I will ruin everything, she kept telling herself silently.

'Is there anything else I can do to help?' she asked sweetly. A cunning plan had formulated in her mind. 'I imagine you will be receiving some important guests at your castle today from what I have heard. Perhaps you would like me to tidy your chamber so it is ready to receive guests?'

'Yes, I've been so busy making plans for the execution that I had not thought about receiving guests in here. Go ahead and tidy.' He watched her as she busied herself, liking what he saw more and more each time they met.

Aislinn kept busy with general tidying, her eyes scanning the room for the Dark Lord's treasure chest. Eventually she spotted it in the corner of his chamber securely locked. She stole a quick glance at him and sure enough, the key was around his neck.

Tap, tap, tap. A knock on the door caused her to raise her eyes.

'Come in,' bellowed Legion in a voice that sounded cheerful even for him.

'Master, you seem in good spirits. I hear that plans are going well for you?'

'Wizard Falstaff,' exclaimed the Dark Lord. 'Back from the druids already? What can you tell me about those keys?'

Aislinn kept her ears tuned while appearing busy with her work.

'Very interesting,' said Falstaff glancing briefly at her. He looked at the Dark Lord unsure whether to continue with this stranger in the room.

'It's all right Falstaff,' he continued sensing his unease with Aislinn in the room. 'You can speak freely.'

'It appears those keys are the keys to life and death and that they hold amazing powers. The problem is how to unlock those powers. The druids are not sure, but they are working on a solution. One thing is certain though – they are extremely valuable and should be protected with all you are worth.'

'Hmmm...,' said Legion thoughtfully. 'Perhaps keeping them here in my treasure chest without protection is not wise. I have a very important scroll in there too that I intend to use in the future. Perhaps we should move this chest to the west tower and place Draco inside to protect it. No one will dare attack a dragon to retrieve it.'

'That is wise, Master,' Falstaff concurred. 'Hopefully the druids will have an answer for us soon.'

Aislinn finished her task and exited the chamber. Her heart was pounding with what she had heard, but it also made it impossible to get hold of the keys Regent needed. Why couldn't things get easier? It seemed new challenges mounted at each turn.

⌘

Aedan met with the Great One – their plan of action was risky and heartbreaking, but it had to unfold this way. There would be too many people lost if they attacked the castle in daylight - they had to attack at night. The Great One knew Ziah would be dead then, but he also knew that this was the only way to ultimately defeat Sephtis. He needed to let the Dark Lord believe that he had won and in so doing he would take that victory and turn it on its head.

Aedan broke the news to the others. 'We will go to the execution posing as travellers who are there to feast. While everyone is distracted with the execution, Mac and

Imogene, you must use this opportunity to find that scroll and your children and free them. You are to escape down the secret tunnel. We don't want any risk to your children when we attack later.'

'But that means Ziah will die?' Imogene posed the question no one else wanted to.

Aedan smiled reassuringly at her.

'Don't worry Imogene, it will be all right.'

Each had a heavy heart for their beloved friend Ziah and none of them understood how things could ever be all right again.

⌘

The executioner and his team of torturers were also busy preparing themselves for the afternoon's events. They sharpened their swords and axes and checked the chains to make sure they were strong and sturdy. Their tools looked frightening. There were sharp steel hooks and tools that could gouge your eyes or intestines out. The rack they used to lay their victim upon was checked and oiled. This would be used to stretch the victim's torso and dislocate their body parts little by little. It was a cruel and evil torture designed to bring a very slow and painful death to the unlucky victim.

⌘

The girls returned to the tower for lunch where they would stay locked up for the remainder of the day. The sadistic side of Legion wanted to make them watch the execution, but his reason to try and win them over won in the end and he knew if he enforced this, they would hate him forever and he would lose the ground he felt he had gained. He falsely believed that Aislinn was being won over as she was showing an interest in him and she was sweet and kind.

Arriving back in the tower, Aislinn rushed to Struan's side. To her dismay she discovered that his fever had soared and he was delirious again.

'No,' she cried. 'I don't believe it – not again!'

She found the cloth and wiped his face gently. He really needed help. If these wounds weren't properly cared for they would become gangrenous and he would die.

She felt his presence even before she heard Maddy squeal in delight.

'Regent!'

'Hello little friend,' he said affectionately to Maddy, scooping her up in his arms and spinning her around.

'Regent,' Aislinn said worriedly. 'Struan needs help. He can't go much longer without it.'

'I know,' he said, 'and help is on its way.'

'What do you mean?'

'During the execution today, you will be rescued, so be ready,' he warned.

'Who is coming for us?' Aislinn asked, extremely curious now.

'That I can't tell you,' Regent replied. 'Now did you find out anything more regarding that key?'

'Yes, but it's not good news I'm afraid. The Dark Lord has discovered from the druids how important the keys are, so he has sent his treasure chest up to the west tower to be guarded by a dragon called Draco.'

'Now that is a nuisance,' said Regent, 'but not an impossibility.'

'Surely fighting a dragon is impossible!' she exclaimed.

'Nothing is impossible for those who believe,' he smiled at her.

'But how will you fight it?' she challenged.

'Not all battles have to be won by physical strength you know,' he said. 'Sometimes just outwitting your enemy can make all the difference. A dragon is not the smartest creature. It is well known that dragons have a vulnerable spot and that is where we need to focus our attack.'

'Where is it?' Maddy asked, totally enraptured by the tale of dragons and battle. She did not quite understand that it was reality they were talking about.

'The vulnerable spot is between his eyes. A dragon has a small horn between the eyes and when it is pierced, it makes him blind.'

'How on earth are you going to get close enough to pierce it?' Aislinn asked. 'It's not like you'll be able to wander in and ask him to sit still while you thump him on the head.'

They all giggled at the thought of this, the laughter medicine to them all. The more they tried to contain it, the more it welled up inside of them and flowed out of their bellies in peals of laughter. Tears ran down their cheeks and they clutched their stomachs as though they were in pain. It was the best thing that had happened to them in a while.

'Enough already,' Regent said trying to be sober, as they all burst into laughter again.

CHAPTER 18

# RESCUE

*I know for sure that loves saves me and that it is here to save us all*

— Maya Angelou

A CONSTANT flow of people streamed into the castle as the hour of the execution drew near. Travellers and villagers from throughout the kingdom, curious about this traitor and the promise of a feast ventured out. It was not often the Dark Lord was generous enough to offer a feast to his subjects; it was an opportunity many would not miss.

In the dungeon Ziah heard the preparations being made for his execution. He had been mocked and jeered by the guards and they relished telling him about the torture and death that awaited him later in the day.

'You are doomed,' some of them shouted at him.

'Only an idiot would turn down power from the Dark Lord. Your brains must have been scrambled when we beat you,' they laughed.

'Good thing too,' another interjected. 'You won't want your wits about you when they begin to torture you.'

Ziah turned away, trying to shut out their chanting and mocking.

'Father,' he whispered, 'I'm not sure where you are, but I trust you completely to do what is best for everyone in our kingdom. If you can, please rescue me but if that is not possible then please give me strength to endure what is coming. I love you.'

Ziah knew his father well. He knew his father would act out of wisdom in this circumstance. As he reflected he became aware of Ryder in the corner of his cell.

'How are you doing Ziah?' he asked.

'Ryder, it's good to see you my friend.'

'We have tried to get your keys but there is no chance of that right now as the Dark Lord has them securely guarded.'

'What does my father say?'

'He wants you to know that he loves you and that no matter what you endure today you will be victorious. Most of all, he wants to know if you will trust him?'

'I trust him – even with my life.'

⌘

Struan continued to weaken and his face began to pale further. His breathing was ragged and shallow, his skin cold and clammy. Aislinn knew the end was coming soon and she cried out to the Great One for mercy. For the first time she felt as though he were not there.

Mac, Imogene, Nuada, Morgan and Aedan entered the castle gates together with a number of other curious villagers and travellers. They looked around and found themselves a place where Mac and Imogene would be able to slip off unnoticed into a courtyard that would lead them to the south side of the castle. They had no idea where to look for the scroll, but they knew their children were in the south tower as Ryder had passed on this information. They settled themselves down and Mac peered into his saddlebag to check that he had brought his special glasses, ring and oil. They would definitely need these to safely release the children. The buzz of excitement in the castle sickened them, but to appear part of the mass group they had to join in and pretend to be excited at the afternoon's events. The great courtyard filled up – every inch with morbid onlookers.

Legion preened and admired himself in his mirror. He wore his finest clothing and a cloak that made him appear more fearsome than he was. This was the moment of his glory - he hoped the Great One was watching every painful moment of it in that mirror of his. His hatred grew as he thought of the Great One and his hunger to inflict revenge upon him was insatiable.

'Let the games begin,' he said to his reflection in the mirror.

Trumpets blasted and people craned to see the Dark Lord as he appeared on his balcony. They pushed and shoved to get a closer view. Mac and Imogene held back – they had no desire to be recognized as it would ruin all their plans and they would need to slip off as soon as the proceedings got under way. Aedan, Nuada and Morgan moved closer to the torture bench. They wanted Ziah to see them, to draw strength from them in his time of need – he must not feel alone.

A cheer erupted from the crowd.

'Announcing the Master, Legion - the Dark Lord himself,' a herald announced.

Legion waved, arrogance oozing from every pore, smiling at the cheering crowd. Clearly, he was relishing his moment of glory - Aedan clenched his fists. His eyes turned to sparkling emerald, his hair glinting in red fury.

'Calm down,' Nuada whispered to him, 'you'll draw attention to us with your hair blazing like that. The time will come when you will have an opportunity to face him.'

'I'm looking forward to that,' he whispered hoarsely.

'Welcome everyone. It is not every day in Griswold where we find ourselves confronted by things that are contrary to our values and beliefs. I have a duty to protect every single one of my subjects from this deception that has tried to invade our kingdom. As your Master I swear to keep you safe from this heresy – to make this a place where we all abide by the rules so that we can live harmoniously side by side. When a stranger comes into our midst and threatens the Lord of Griswold, then it has to be dealt with accordingly.'

'Hooray,' shouted the crowd, deceived by the Dark Lord's words.

'The only one who is speaking heresy is you,' Aedan growled under his breath.

He looked over at Nuada who looked sick with anger. His parents had been threatened and killed by this evil man – he was falsely condemning Ziah for the very thing he had done. *He's a hypocrite.*

'Who would like to see the prisoner?' He stirred the crowd further.

'Bring out the prisoner.'

'Kill him, we don't want traitors in Griswold,' others chanted.

The doors to the dungeon opened and Ziah was dragged out in chains. The crowd erupted as though they were at a sport meeting.

'Traitor, traitor' - the word reverberated around the castle walls like a clanging gong.

Ziah squinted, the light blinding him after the dingy dungeon. He looked bewildered to see so many people who knew nothing about him willing to condemn him on the word of the Dark Lord.

*So much for justice and innocent until proven guilty*, he thought.

Mac and Imogene slipped through the door leading to the next courtyard while the crowd focused on Ziah's entrance. No one noticed them leave. Mac put on the glasses so as to be ready for any unexpected surprises. They looked around momentarily trying to get their bearings.

'Which way is it to the south tower?' Imogene asked Mac.

'I think it's this way,' he replied entering a door to the castle. 'So far I don't see anyone but we still need to be cautious.'

They made their way through the draughty halls staying close to the wall, keeping their ears tuned to any approaching people. This place was a mausoleum – so different to Lionsgate and they shivered at the thought of living here.

'We need to find the stairs which will take us to the south tower,' he said frustrated. 'I can't work it out. It looked so simple from the outside but I'm not sure now. There are too many passages and corridors.'

'Shh...' Imogene cautioned. 'Someone's coming.'

They looked for a place to hide and found a curtained recess in the wall. Silently they hid behind the curtain, feeling as though their pounding hearts could be heard echoing all through the halls.

'Come on woman,' the old man said. 'You always make us late for things and I don't want to miss the execution.'

'I'm sorry Morris,' her voice sullen, 'but I couldn't just leave those children without any refreshment all day. Once the feasting begins they will be forgotten and they'll get hungry and thirsty.'

'Maureen, I've told you a hundred times not to get attached to them. They are not your responsibility and the time may come when they are of no use, then where will you be if the Dark Lord disposes of them?'

Imogene clasped her hand over her mouth, a moan escaping from her throat. The thought of the Dark Lord disposing of her children was unthinkable. She knew they had to get them out tonight – it was their only chance.

Mac had seen through the curtain with his magic glasses where the old couple had alighted from. If they had seen the children then that was the route to follow. Once they knew the corridor was clear they slipped out following the direction they had come from. They soon found a strong wooden door that led to a stairwell.

'This must be it,' he whispered in excitement. 'Let's get our children Imogene.'

It felt like the longest climb they had ever taken and they were relieved to finally get to the top of the stairs. A number of doors led off the top of the stairwell.

'How do we know which door it is?' Imogene cried in dismay.

'Imogene – you forget,' he said pointing to his spectacles, reminding her of the fantastic glasses he was wearing.

Behind the first door was an empty room that looked musty and derelict. The second door housed excess furniture that was not being used in the castle.

'This is it,' Mac shouted triumphantly at the third door. 'I can see Maddy and Aislinn,' he said choking back tears of joy and relief. He pushed the glasses onto the top of his head as they misted up with his tears.

They tried the door but found it locked – a frustrating barrier to the reunion they so longed for.

'How are we going to get in?'

'I'm not sure, but we haven't come this far to let a locked door deter us,' he said with determination. 'Let's look around and see if we can find a key. There must be a key for whoever brings the children food and water.'

They searched around the door frame feeling above the door ledge, alongside the door for a nail or hook that would perhaps hold the key, to no avail.

'It's no good,' Imogene cried, tears bristling at the side of her eyes.

'There's got to be a way.' He pulled down the glasses and looked carefully around the door. 'I see the key behind these stones Imogene,' he whispered excitedly but they had no way of knowing how to get access to it.

'This can't be happening,' Mac said angrily punching the wall where the key was. He felt helpless and frustrated.

To their delight the punch activated a mechanism and the wall shifted and creaked as though the stones were being re-arranged. A cavity opened and there before them was the key.

⌘

Ziah stood chained to a post as the crowds hissed and spat at him. He noticed Aedan, Nuada and Morgan as he had been brought in and they nodded ever so slightly as he passed them. It gave him courage to undergo this torture and to see this through to the end- whatever that may be.

'Why doesn't he retaliate?' Nuada asked under his breath. 'He's the Great One's son after all and has powers the Dark Lord could only dream of. He could save himself.'

'Hush,' Aedan said. 'He does not have his keys any more Nuada, but the Great One has another plan in mind. Ziah will buy us time to release the children by sacrificing himself to let the Dark Lord think he has the victory. That's all I can say for now – we can't talk here – it's too risky.'

Ziah endured abuse after abuse never once defending himself, the crowds frenzied in their behaviour.

'So...' Legion roared from his seat on the balcony, 'you don't seem so sure of yourself anymore young man. Where is this army you threatened me with earlier? It seems as though you have been deserted. Perhaps your father doesn't quite value you as much as you thought. I don't see him rushing in here to rescue you.'

The crowd cheered and laughed at his cuckolding.

He raised his hand and a hush fell over the people.

Are you ready to surrender to me yet Ziah – there is still that opportunity we spoke of earlier today?'

'I would rather die than surrender to you,' Ziah spat.

'Your wish is my command - then die you shall.'

A herald raised his trumpet to his lips, blasting it ceremoniously before reading from the parchment the Dark Lord handed him.

'Ziah, you've been found guilty of trying to deceive these good people to follow another, and as such are a traitor to the kingdom of Griswold. The punishment for your crime is death by torture.'

The words of finality hung thick in the air, the crowd leaning forward, blood thirsty vampires.

'Let the punishment begin,' declared Legion with a glint of victory in his eyes. *I hope you are watching Old Man – and I hope it kills you!*

⌘

Mac fumbled with the key. The faster he tried, the clumsier he felt. Eventually he took a deep breath and slowed his steadying hand to work methodically. The key slipped in smoothly and clicked as he turned it. They pushed the door open and rushed in to see Aislinn, with chair in hand, ready to protect Maddy from the intruders. It took a few seconds for her to register who she was looking at.

'Papa, Mama!' she exclaimed disbelievingly, 'We thought you were dead...' She could say no more as the weight of all she had endured came to a climax - tears poured down her face.

They wrapped the girls in their arms as though they would never let go.

'Sorry to interrupt this reunion,' echoed a voice behind them.

Mac swung around ready to tackle the intruder. No one would separate his family again. Aislinn recognized the look of fear and anger on her father's face.

'Wait Papa, this is Regent. He's from the Great One - he is the Protector of Royalty. He and his friends have helped us by keeping us safe.'

Mac's countenance changed and he stretched out his hand to the stranger.

'Then I thank you,' he said with genuine emotion in his voice.

Imogene noticed Struan lying on the bed and that he was not well.

'Mac, Struan has a fever and looks extremely poor.' The concern in her voice worried him.

'Yes, Mama, he has an infection in the wounds on his hands. I've tried to keep them clean and his fever down, but it has not helped.'

'You've done well Aislinn,' her mother commended her.

Imogene was so consumed with her oldest son she had not noticed that her youngest was absent from the tower room. It dawned on her slowly, that something was not right.

'Mitchell! Where's Mitchell, Aislinn?'

Her daughter's stricken face spoke a thousand words and Imogene's heart sank. She assumed the worst.

'I'm sorry Mama, I tried, but I couldn't stop them. They took him and gave him to one of the Dark Lord's wizards.'

'Nooo,' the anguished cry escaped from deep within her belly.

Her mind ran, out of control - she imagined her little boy being given as a sacrifice to the Dark Lord.

'We'll get him back Mama,' she pleaded, feeling guilt suffocate her.

Aislinn chastised herself for not protecting Mitchell better. She tried to reassure her mother but felt that no matter what she said it would not take away the crushing guilt she felt.

'I'm sure she will take care of him, she has wanted a child for so long. We'll get him back I promise Mama.'

Aislinn's desperate words sank in as Imogene realized that he had not been taken for sacrifice.

'Tell me everything you know,' she whispered urgently.

'Imogene, Aislinn – we must get out of here now, Struan needs immediate help and if we delay any longer we may be discovered. We will not be able to help Mitchell if we are all prisoners of the Dark Lord,' Mac urged.

Imogene mentally shook herself. He was right – they had to think of their other three children and get them to safety before they were discovered. Just when she thought this whole awful mess was coming to an end there seemed to be another twist and turn. Would this nightmare ever end?

# CHAPTER 19

# SACRIFICE

*A man who was completely innocent, offered himself as a sacrifice*
*for the good of others, including his enemies, and became the ransom of*
*the world. It was a perfect act*

— Mahatma Gandhi

ZIAH was exhausted – he had been beaten, mocked and ridiculed. Now he lay tied to the rack like an animal ready for slaughter. His hair was plastered to his forehead, a mixture of sweat, matted blood and grime. Although his body looked beaten and broken, his eyes were determined and fiery. The skies above the castle darkened as thick black clouds rolled in - even the forces of nature recognized the injustice of this ridiculous trial. Dust blew in small eddying circles in the courtyard and people covered their noses and mouths with their tunics as nature protested fiercely at the day's events.

The torturers stretched out Ziah's body by turning the wooden handle on the bench. A jarring, scraping noise could be heard as the bench moved apart inch by inch.

Ziah was determined to go through this pain with as much dignity as possible. He gritted his teeth and endured the pain of his arms and legs being pulled apart - it felt as though he was being torn into pieces – muscle by muscle. The pain was excruciating and every now and again when he passed out from the unbearable agony of it all, the torturers would fill their buckets and throw icy water over his face. Then the whole awful process would begin again.

Legion was enjoying himself. He was disappointed that the weather was marring his fun, but seeing Ziah powerless and pathetic brought him more pleasure than could be imagined.

'So Great One,' he muttered to himself, 'I hope you're watching and feeling as wretched as I felt when you banished me from your kingdom. Pain is not pleasant now, is it?'

The torture continued and became so cruel that many women and children had to turn away from the brutality of it all.

Morgan, Nuada and Aedan never once looked away from Ziah's eyes. Their eyes sent him messages of courage and love as their tears flowed freely.

⌘

Mac and Imogene had a decision to make regarding Struan.

'Give him some of the oil. It will heal him Mac.'

'I know,' Mac said, 'but if we use even a drop then we will not be able to use it if one of us is killed during our escape. Remember what the Great One said about using it wisely.'

'But he could die!' she cried anguished.

'I know, Imogene,' he said gently, 'but if that happens and we have all the oil we can bring him back to life with it. Do you trust the Great One's words?' he asked her.

She hesitated only for a fraction of a second and then nodded her head, realizing the logic of his argument.

'Now we need to find the scroll.'

Aislinn raised her head at the mention of the scroll.

'The Dark Lord has an important scroll but he's locked it away together with Ziah's keys in the west tower. It's guarded by a ferocious dragon,' she said.

'Great!' muttered Mac under his breath.

'Let's get out of here for now,' Regent suggested. 'We need to get the children to safety first and formulate a plan for getting the scroll and keys back later.'

Mac scooped Struan into his arms, placed the glasses firmly on his face and headed for the door with Imogene and Maddy close behind.

As they exited the door, Aislinn cried, 'Wait...'

She rushed back into the room, fumbled in the pillowslip. She pulled out her gemstone and feather. She would always keep them with her as a reminder of this adventure and one day she would tell her children all about it.

With the help of the magical glasses they made their way down the tower stairs without any problems. In the hallway of the castle they found a coat rack full of cloaks.

'Take a cloak for Aislinn and Maddy, and another to cover Struan otherwise they may be recognized and your escape hindered,' Regent suggested.

'Yes, it's a good plan,' Mac agreed. They placed the cloaks around the girls so that they would look like any other traveling family that day. Imogene covered Struan's weak body with another cloak. Perhaps they could pass him off as a sleeping child being carried by his father after a long, tiring day.

'I must leave you now,' said Regent, 'but we will see each other again.'

Aislinn and Maddy both hugged him, thanking him for being there for them.

'I'll always be around, don't you worry,' he chuckled.

They left the castle hall and headed for the stables and the secret tunnel that would lead to their freedom.

Imogene hated leaving without Mitchell, but her first priority was to see her other children to safety. They needed a plan as to how they would get their little boy back.

They passed through the courtyard and slowly made their way around the crowds that were pressing in to see Ziah's final humiliation.

'Don't look,' Mac whispered to Aislinn and Maddy as they passed through the courtyard. He had no desire for his children to witness any more of the Dark Lord's evil and brutality.

They headed for the stables, hoping no one would notice them or stop them. As they entered the stable, a young guard blocked their entrance.

'Where are you going?' he asked gruffly.

'We are looking for a place to rest the wee ones,' Mac replied pointing to Maddy and what appeared to be a sleeping Struan. 'We've had a long journey today and the children are worn out.'

'Aye,' said the guard, 'there's an empty stall at the end of the stable. They can rest there if you like.'

'Thank you,' said Imogene gratefully.

Slowly they made their way to the stall he had pointed out to them. They would have to wait for an opportune moment to escape down the secret tunnel - patience would need to be exercised.

Mac settled the children in the stall, waiting for the guard to move off. He did not budge but remained in the entrance of the stables.

'This could be a long wait,' Mac whispered to Imogene. They were so close to freedom, it was unbearable.

A loud cheer erupted and chants of 'Kill him' rang out through the crowd. The guard's curiosity got the better of him. He stepped out of the stables, craning his neck to see what was taking place.

'Now,' said Mac to his family. 'We need to move now!'

⌘

The air was charged with evil and Ziah knew that the end was near. He had endured torture that was beyond cruel and yet still he trusted his father. He looked up into the sky, his body stretched out in the shape of a crucifix as he was laid out on the rack. He smiled at the angry sky, a raindrop falling onto his cheek like a tear from the heavens. He knew he was not alone and that he was loved. Aedan, his precious friend was there for him and his father was close by –he could feel it. He knew too, that the Hamilton children would be free by now and his heart rejoiced in that.

In a final act of defiance his voice rang out strong through the courtyard, 'Forgive them father – I'm coming home.'

Legion was caught completely unaware by this declaration. Silence descended upon the courtyard as the shocked onlookers heard those words.

'What did he say…?' he growled under his breath to his advisors.

He was more than annoyed with this final act of bravado. He raised his hand to the executioner and let it fall swiftly to his side.

At his signal, the executioner picked up a stake, raised it above his head and brought it down quickly, piercing Ziah's heart in one motion. The crowd gasped, then began to cheer. In their minds a traitor had been justly punished.

Legion sensed his victory was complete although it was marred by Ziah's final declaration.

'Clean up the mess, tonight we feast for Griswold is safe.'

He stood up, looked once more at Ziah's lifeless corpse, his blood seeping into the earth below the torture slab, and headed back to his chambers to savour his victory.

Aedan, Nuada and Morgan could not move from where they were standing. They were devastated at the brutality of Ziah's death and were in shock.

'We can't leave him here,' Nuada said, broken. 'He deserves better than that.'

'How are we going to take him without arousing suspicion?' Morgan asked.

'No, we need to leave him for now,' Aedan declared. 'This battle is not over yet – we retrieve him tonight from the castle.'

The three men made their way to the stable with the secret passage. They did not want to appear to be leaving the castle for fear of attracting attention as most travelers were staying for the great feast that night.

Quickly and quietly they left the castle via the hidden tunnel to report all they had seen.

CHAPTER 20

# RESTORATION

*The work of restoration cannot begin until a problem is fully faced*

— Dan B. Allender

IMOGENE and Mac were extremely worried about Struan now. His body was listless and clammy and his wounds seeped infectious toxins. They lay him down as comfortably as they could and Imogene bathed his brow and redressed his wounds.

As they attended to their son, they became aware of another father suffering - anguished at the plight of his own son.

'Great One,' Mac said softly as he noticed him watching them take care of their son. 'Thank you for helping us to save our children. If it wasn't for you and Ziah, they would not be with us now.'

'I'm delighted for you to have your children back again. That is what both Ziah and I wished,' the Great One said genuinely. 'There is no greater love than a parent's for a child.'

He turned away slightly - Mac did not miss the pain in his voice.

'I pray you will get Ziah back,' Imogene added, although she knew that the chances of him being alive were impossible.

'Oh, I will get him back,' the Great One said. 'No matter what has happened I'll have him back with me and will not leave him in Sephtis' hands. He thinks he has won this battle, but there is so much he has not perceived yet.'

Imogene and Mac were not sure what the Great One was referring to. They hoped the strain of the day's events had not caused him to lose his faculties. Still, they had never known the Great One to be overcome by circumstances and they believed that he would be victorious again in this battle. They had no idea how that would happen but they trusted him more than anything in the world.

The Great One had done so much for them – now they realized they could do something for him. Imogene reached into the leather pouch and pulled out the oil. This could bring Ziah back if they could get his body. Mac nodded in agreement, aware of what his wife was thinking. Ziah had sacrificed himself for their children's freedom and now it was their turn. They were well aware that Struan might not make it through the night and it pained them both. Far more was at stake than just their family. The loss of Ziah would have great ramifications and impact throughout Griswold and the kingdoms beyond. He was the Key Keeper and no one else could use those keys but him. Without him the land was doomed to bondage and freedom would no longer be a choice for people. He had sacrificed himself for their children, now they needed to sacrifice the oil to save him. They had to trust that Struan would make it through this ordeal. This defeat would be the answer to bringing liberty not only to themselves, but to many others living under the condemnation and wrath of the Dark Lord. Mac took the vial of oil from Imogene and stretched out his hand to the Great One offering the precious gift to him.

'I would not ask this of you,' the Great One said, 'as I understand what it is to lose a son. Are you sure you want to make this choice, as it must be your choice and no one else's. I will not hold it against you if you use this on your son – I gave it to you to use as you will.'

'We are certain of one thing only,' Mac said softly but with steely determination in his voice. 'We have trusted and given our lives for you Great One and you have never failed us, even in the hard and painful times. We trust you more than ever and now we have met Ziah and Aedan, we never want to be without them. We finally understand what true love and community is.'

'Ah yes,' the Great One said wistfully. 'My kingdom is not about rules, nor is it a place like Lionsgate – my kingdom is about people and more importantly about love It's a pity so few men get to experience it as you have recently. This is a treasure that has been discovered by you and your family and it is to be held fast to your hearts. When you see more clearly through new eyes, you can never go back to being the same ever again as you will find out in time Mac. Thank you for this gift,' He said indicating the healing oil.

A groan escaped from Struan's lips, bringing them back to the reality of the situation. Imogene rushed to his side, cradling him, whispering words of strength and love into his ear.

'You can do this Struan,' she encouraged, 'fight it with all you've got; we're here now and won't leave you again.'

The Great One smiled at her courage as he quietly slipped away into the night.

It was a night of heartbreak for Imogene - she had lost one son and she was terrified that she might lose the other before the night was out.

The girls lay huddled together in a makeshift tent that had been erected in the trees, hidden from the roadside and curious eyes. There was still the danger that the Dark Lord may discover they were gone and send out a search party to look for them. The others hoped the feasting would be long and flowing with wine which would keep them from noticing the Hamilton children's absence.

Aedan, Nuada and Morgan discussed the plan to recover Ziah's body and the other possessions the Dark Lord had stolen.

'Tonight is the night,' Aedan declared. 'If we leave it any longer there will not be another opportunity.'

'Aye,' Nuada agreed. 'The feasting will cause enough of a diversion for us to be able to get him out.'

It was decided that they would return to the Dark Lord's castle once the feasting was well under way.

'Get everyone ready,' Aedan declared – 'we go to get our dear brother, Ziah.'

The men readied themselves, arming themselves with weapons that could easily be concealed. They carried a cloak made of gold and purple cloth which they planned to wrap Ziah's broken body in.

'Is Mac ready to leave yet,' Nuada asked Imogene. It had been decided that Imogene would stay with Struan and the children to care for them.

'Yes, I'm ready – let's do it.'

A voice broke into the conversation. It was Aislinn. 'I'm going with you Papa,' she declared.

'No, Aislinn,' he answered equally as firmly. 'You need to be here to help your mother. Besides, it's far too dangerous.'

'Papa, I have suffered more than you could know over the last few days and everything that was precious to me was stolen. I can be of great help to you. I know the castle better than any of you and I know the Dark Lord's chambers because I've seen them. I may be young, but I know evil when I see it, and the Dark Lord is evil itself. I've cared for Maddy and Struan and protected them as best I could and I think I have proved I am responsible.'

Her steely gaze took both Mac and Imogene by surprise. Something else had been stolen by The Dark Lord – their daughter's innocence and naivety - she would never be the same again.

With resignation Mac nodded his head and Aislinn joined the group. His daughter could be very stubborn when she wanted to, but she was right, she did know the castle better than any of them.

'Time to go,' Aedan said. 'We'll look after her Imogene – don't worry.'

The band of warriors made their way through the tunnel, silence hanging over them like a thick veil. Each was alone with their thoughts and each imagined what was to come.

Approaching the end of the tunnel they noticed a man with a travelling cloak over his head and shoulders. He appeared to be waiting for them and immediately they were on their guard ready to war if necessary. Had the Dark Lord discovered the Hamilton children's disappearance? Were they keeping watch at all the entrances for attack?

'Put down your weapons,' the voice said. 'It's just me.'

A chuckle erupted from Aedan.

'I should have known you would come,' he said to the older man.

The Great One removed the cloak from his head, hugging Aedan fiercely.

'Thank you for being with Ziah at the end,' he said. 'I know it would have given him courage and strength. Nothing will keep me from being with him now – It's time to turn Sephtis' victory on its head.'

They decided on their plan of action. They would find Ziah and retrieve his body. Then they would head into the castle to find the west tower and the treasure box that contained the Keys of the Kingdom and the scroll. Once they had these items, they would head back to the forest and ready themselves to return home. The hope was that the feasting would continue way into the night and that no one would notice that Ziah or the Hamilton children were gone till the morning. There was a lot to be accomplished in one night and the risk was very great but this would be their only opportunity.

Entering the stable they could hear the revelry taking place with all the feasting. Loud, drunken voices echoed through the courtyard and giggling could be heard occasionally too as maidens attended to the merry men. Nuada and Aedan wandered out of the stable, hanging onto one another like two drunkards holding each other up.

Approaching some of the men in the courtyard, they pretended to be intoxicated with the free flowing wine.

'Aye good evening, gentleman,' Nuada said loudly. 'What a feast this has been. I think I need to thank the poor sod who got himself mutilated today, for thanks to him we have a belly full of food and more wine than we need.'

The others laughed equally loudly.

'Well then, I guess you should,' replied a gruff man who clearly was struggling to stand upright. 'He's been put out on display for all to see at the gate to the castle as a reminder that traitors die nasty deaths.' He waved his arm wildly in the direction of the gate, almost losing his balance with the vigorous gesture.

Nuada and Aedan continued to distract the revellers as the others moved stealthily toward the gate looking for Ziah's body. Just inside the entrance to the castle they found him tied up against a post, his head hanging limply on his bruised and bloodied body. There were no guards.

'If we take him down, someone will notice he has gone,' Morgan said thoughtfully.

'Alerting them to our presence before we are ready is not a good thing.'

'Yes, we need to get in and out without anyone noticing us,' The Great One said.

They looked about to see if they were attracting attention but all that could be seen was a rat or two seeking leftovers from the feast. In the corner of the castle courtyard they noticed a young man who had overindulged in the feasting. His body was slumped against the wall and he was gently snoring as he slept off the considerable amount of wine he had consumed.

'Perfect!' Morgan chuckled, mischief in his eyes. 'It looks like we have a scapegoat to keep our cover.'

Effortlessly he lifted up the sleeping man who merely grunted as he was moved. The Great One untied Ziah and caught him to his breast. The young drunkard was placed against the post as Mac quickly tied him up. Every now and again he would mutter something under his breath before settling back into his stupor. He must have consumed a vast quantity of wine.

'Hopefully they won't notice in the dark that it's not Ziah,' Morgan said, 'but just to be sure we need to make it more convincing.'

Morgan pulled out a long knife and Aislinn caught her breath in surprise and shock. She watched fearfully as he lifted the knife dreading what he might be about to do.

Morgan lifted his hand and neatly sliced a large cut across his palm. Immediately his blood flowed and he proceeded to wipe it across the young man's face and clothing, disguising him as the beaten and bloody Ziah. Then he quickly wrapped his hand in a handkerchief to stem the blood flow.

'No pain, no gain,' he quipped smiling sweetly at Aislinn.

The Great One carefully and lovingly carried his son across the courtyard and into the stable to find some privacy. He needed to be alone with Ziah. He knelt over his son as he lay still and cold upon the straw in the humble stable. The Great One had known his son was going to die and that it would be brutal and vicious as he knew the nature of the Dark Lord. It had to be so for the Hamilton children to be saved. Ziah had embraced evil and death with strength and dignity and his father was proud of him. He thought of how Mac and Imogene laid down their hope of Struan being saved by giving him the healing oil for Ziah.

He gently bent his head over his son.

Mac, Aislinn and Morgan finished their task of tying up the young man. They made their way over to where Nuada and Aedan were 'celebrating' with the revellers. Morgan quickly gave an owl hoot – the signal that they were ready to take on the next part of their mission. At the signal Nuada and Aedan readied themselves to leave.

'Well brothers,' Nuada said, 'we think that more wine calls and maybe even a cute serving wench,' he winked as they stumbled off toward the courtyard.

They could hear the men making lewd remarks as they left, roaring with laughter.

'They will certainly have very painful heads tomorrow,' Aedan smiled.

As they met up with the others, they saw the Great One alight from the stable. A golden glow emanated from the interior of the stable, his face reflecting love and sheer joy.

Mac and Aislinn gasped, as did Nuada and Morgan, as a figure was silhouetted in the doorway to the stable. Ziah! His personality filled the courtyard.

'Ziah,' Aislinn whispered, 'how can it be possible?'

'All things are possible for those who believe,' a familiar voice whispered to her as she looked up into the smiling eyes of Regent. She remembered his earlier words and nodded her head in agreement.

'Yes, everything is possible,' she declared.

'Welcome back brother,' Aedan said to Ziah, grasping him in a manly embrace. 'I've been waiting in eager expectation to see you again.'

The question in Mac and Aislinn's eyes made the Great One smile even more broadly.

'This was part of the plan,' the Great One said.

'You planned Ziah's death?' Mac asked incredulously, a little shocked that the Great One would do such a thing to his own son.

'No Mac. The Dark Lord did that because he is evil. I would never choose to hurt my son because I love him so greatly. That is why we changed the plan. We know that evil will never overcome goodness if there are people to fight it and people who stand against it as you all have done. We knew that Ziah's death and return to life would distress the Dark Lord and cause turmoil – he will learn that goodness in people is far more powerful than intimidating them with fear. Now we must find those keys and that scroll before it is too late.'

Mac nodded remembering the healing oil he had given the Great One to use on Ziah. He quickly sent up a prayer for Struan. The Great One knew his turmoil and loved him even more at that moment

# CHAPTER 21
## DECEPTION

*Appear weak when you are strong, and strong when you are weak*
— Sun Tzu, The Art of War

LEGION was pleased. His feast had gone well, he had crippled the Great One and it gave him great satisfaction. He no longer looked like a fool – the people of Griswold knew he was a formidable ruler and that he was powerful too. He excused himself from the feasting, encouraging his wizards and goblins to keep feasting. He wanted to be alone to savour his victory and plan his next move. He made his way up to the west tower. He wanted his treasure box- he felt confident and safe enough to retrieve them. He needed to read that scroll again –to formulate a plan that would forever keep those children bound to him. He had to ensure that above all else, they did not become like their parents. He was relieved Mac and Imogene were dead but he also knew their children had grown up with their values and that was what he needed to kill. He had taken care of the little one – he would grow up in the home of Morelock and learn magic that would benefit the Dark Lord. As for Aislinn he was so attracted to her beauty and her spirit. He would tame that spirit and make her his queen. She would be beautiful next to him, if he could break her and mould her. It was a challenge he looked forward to. Never before had he allowed himself to feel emotional about someone. Nonetheless he did feel something for that young girl – he mistook it for love but actually it was the challenge of breaking her feisty spirit and moulding her to his ways that attracted him to her – he did not have the ability to love. He only had the ability to conquer and enslave.

He unlocked the tower door and entered, Draco's sulphuric breath hitting him but even that did not deter Legion.

'Hold back sulphur's flame

You are Draco and you are tame

Release the treasure that is mine

While you slumber for a short time.'

He chanted the spell to ensure his safety from the razor sharp claws and fiery breath.

Immediately the Dragon became complacent and listless. He lay on his back and waited for Legion to scratch his tummy.

'There's no time for that Draco,' he said patting the dragon. 'I have work to do.'

He scooped up the treasure box and headed out the door back to his chamber, leaving the dragon snoring.

⌘

The team of warriors had increased in number and Aislinn felt more secure having Regent and Ryder there too. They made their way up the tower stairs cautiously and quickly, being careful not to bump into anyone. At one point they heard footsteps coming down the tower stairs. They only just managed to find a door leading off the tower which enabled them to hide quietly till the footsteps receded.

'How are we going to overcome the dragon,' Aislinn asked Regent. 'I know he has a vulnerable spot on his head, but how will we get to it?'

'Don't worry about it,' he smiled, 'where there's a will there's a way.'

'You haven't seen Aedan deal with thieves yet,' Mac chuckled.

At the door to the tower Mac put his glasses on again and looked through the thick metal door.

'I see the dragon,' he said. 'He appears very large, but if I'm not mistaken, he is fast asleep and does not appear to be guarding anything.'

'Can you see the treasure box?' Aislinn asked. 'It's made of carved wood with silver laid into it.'

Mac scanned his eyes across the room.

'No, I don't see anything except the dragon. Are you sure this is the room?' he asked.

'Yes,' Regent and Aislinn replied simultaneously.

'Where would he move it to?' Ryder asked.

'There's only one place it can be if it is not here,' Aislinn said earnestly, 'and that is back with the Dark Lord. He would not entrust it to anyone else.'

'It makes perfect sense,' the Great One said. 'He most certainly would want to gloat over his treasures and now he feels confident enough to have them with him. Where is his chamber Aislinn?'

The group made their way back down the tower stairs and to the Dark Lord's chamber. Occasionally they would have to find a place to hide and conceal themselves from people passing in the drafty corridors, but most people were tired from feasting or too intoxicated to care about the strangers in the castle.

'Let me go into the Dark Lord's chamber to see if the treasure box is there? Aislinn asked the Great One.

'No Aislinn, It's far too dangerous.' Mac could not bear the thought of losing her again.

'Papa, the Dark Lord trusts me in his chamber, and I can say that I was sent to make sure he has everything he needs before bedtime. He will not be suspicious that we have escaped if he sees me and it will give us more time.'

'That is a very courageous offer young lady,' the Great One smiled, 'but not one we require you to make.'

'I think it makes perfect sense,' Ziah said quietly. 'I trust you Aislinn to do this if you want to, but only if you want to, not because you have to.'

'I do want to Ziah,' she said emphatically. 'I have learned today that we lay down our lives for the ones we love and I love all of you. Besides, Great One, you have just told us that evil will never overcome goodness if there are people to stand up against it. That's what I'm doing.'

'Good girl, but you won't have to lay down your life tonight – we will be here to protect you.'

The others hid in the niches outside the Dark Lord's chamber while Aislinn steeled herself to enter the room.

'Here is something for you to use should you need it,' the Great One said handing her a vial of powder. 'This will send him into a drugged sleep if you get the opportunity to use it, but don't endanger yourself.'

She tucked the vial into her tunic pocket and headed for the chamber. She knocked quietly on the door. At first there was no response and she wondered if he were in there. She knocked again a little louder this time. She heard the frustrated growl of the Dark Lord inside and her heart hammered in her chest.

*Take deep breaths and keep calm*, she thought.

The door was yanked open by Legion. He was ready to abuse whoever was there but when he saw Aislinn he held back the rebuff. What a pleasant surprise.

'Well, well, who do we have here? Are you missing me young Aislinn?' he said sardonically and a little flirtatiously.

'I was sent up to check that you have everything you need before you retire, Sir,' she said sweetly. 'If you like I can add more wood to your fire and turn down your bed for you, or perhaps you would like a little more wine poured?'

The attention of a young and beautiful girl seeing to his comfort was the crowning glory of his victory and the Dark Lord ushered her in. His vanity was piqued.

Regent clenched his fists in fury and anger.

'Did you see the way he was looking at her?' he ranted. 'I'll wipe that smile off his face if he dares lay a hand on her.'

'Calm down Regent,' Ryder said. 'She will be fine.'

'She's good,' Nuada chuckled, 'she has him completely fooled.'

Inside the chamber Aislinn added some wood to the fire all the while scanning the chamber for the treasure box. She did not see it in the seating area of the chamber so she assumed it must be near the Dark Lord's writing desk or next to his bed. She made her way over to the bed to turn down the covers when she felt his stare upon her back. Fear crawled up her spine like a spider up a web and her stomach turned into a knot. Her courage must not fail her now. She spun around, forcing a winsome smile to her lips.

'Would you like more wine, Sir?' she asked praying that he would agree.

'Don't be so formal Aislinn. I would prefer you to call me Legion. I'll have some wine if you join me,' he said eyeing her up and down as though she were a tasty morsel to eat.

'I've never had wine before,' she said, 'but I'm willing to try a little bit if it pleases you Sir... I mean Legion.'

His name rolling off her tongue felt like a mouthful of sticky molasses.

'There are many new experiences I wish to teach you Aislinn – wine is just one of them. Let me pour you some my dear.'

'No Legion,' she said charmingly, 'it is my job to serve you. Why don't you sit down and I will get it for us. It would be an honour for me to serve the master of this castle.'

Legion was completely won over by her flattery. His arrogance and pride clouded his judgement - he allowed himself to believe that this sweet, innocent girl was attracted to his power and wealth. He knew that having power would change his world and this was just the beginning. He added some more wood to the fire then made himself comfortable in the armchair as Aislinn went to pour their drinks. She reached into her pocket and brought the vial out, tipping the contents into his goblet. Then she poured the wine over the powder and prayed that he would not notice it as it dissolved. She poured herself a small goblet of wine and carried it over to the fire near him.

'Sit here with me,' he urged pointing to the chair opposite him. 'I could get used to this Aislinn. I can offer you wealth and prestige if you were by my side.'

Aislinn tried not to choke on her wine in revulsion at the thought. She smiled nervously at him and replied, 'That is very kind sir, but I need time to get to know you first.'

'We have plenty of that he said,' sipping his wine greedily. Making her his queen would be a double arrow to the Great One's heart – the daughter of one of his followers becoming his – how the Great One would hate that – he smiled at the thought.

His eyes began to water and feel blurry. He rubbed them as though he were in a dream and shook his head as though to clear it. He kept seeing more than one of her. What was happening to him? His mind felt foggy and wouldn't work very well. He could hear her chatting to him but he could not make out the words she was saying. Then he was swallowed up in inky blackness!

Aislinn moved quickly, opening the chamber door. She waved to the others who were awaiting her signal. Mac breathed a sigh of relief to see her safe. It was the hardest thing to do, letting her go into that chamber but he was proud of her courage and strength.

They entered and looked around for the treasure box. It was under his bed and after retrieving the key from around his neck they opened it up. Ziah picked up the keys that belonged to him and put them into his tunic pocket. Mac looked into the box, breathing a sigh of relief at the sight of the scroll. He lifted it out and opened it up, his heart aching again as he saw the condemning words inscribed on it. He quickly closed it – he had verified it was the right scroll, but he would never read it again as it was the past - he did not want to relive it. They made their way out of the chamber and headed back to the tunnel. For tonight, they had achieved their goal and won a great victory. The Dark Lord would be furious.

⌘

In the forest Imogene paced up and down restlessly waiting for their return. Maddy had only just gone to sleep – she had been unable to tear herself from the safety of her mother's arms and had eventually fallen asleep curled up in her mother's lap. Struan lay feverishly wrapped in a fur pelt and Imogene had to bathe his forehead every few minutes. She tried to stop herself thinking of all the things that could go wrong.

Her sixth sense kicked in, making her aware of another presence in the forest. She scanned the thicket floor for a large piece of wood, snatching it up to defend her children from any other perils.

'Who's there?' she called out, trying not to sound afraid.

'Don't be afraid,' the voice said.

Imogene strained her eyes to see into the darkness. It was a woman's voice.

She stepped out into the firelight and Imogene caught her breath. She was beautiful, radiating colour and light. She seemed familiar, although Imogene knew that they had never met.

'My name's Serena,' she said to Imogene, continuing, 'I have met your children Aislinn and Maddy.'

Imogene became fearful again. How could this woman have met Maddy and Aislinn - they had been in captivity? Was she one of the Dark Lord's subjects sent out in the guise of beauty to capture them again?

'How can that be?' Imogene asked, still not relinquishing her hold on the wood.

'I met them in the tower of the Dark Lord's,' she said smiling. 'The Great One sent us to encourage them and keep their spirits up.'

'How can I believe you,' she asked, not sure what to do.

'There's nothing I can do to make you believe me, except to ask why you are so afraid to believe that the things you have seen and experienced the last few days are real? The kingdom you visited when you met the Great One is not a dream, nor is it a place you will go to one day, Imogene. It's a place you can go to whenever you need the Great One. He does not want you separated from him by time or space. Your imagination is the key to the door of his kingdom. When you believe you can enter in anytime.'

'How did you know we were there?' Imogene asked.

'Because I come from there,' Serena replied simply.

'Why are you here now?' Imogene asked still suspicious.

'Because I am the Protector of Gifts,' she replied.

'There are no gifts or treasures here,' Imogene said, more suspicious now than ever.

'Imogene, you and the children are the gifts – you are extremely precious to the Great One- he loves you more than you will ever comprehend. Even if you never do another thing for him, it won't change how he feels. You are precious gifts to him and I am here to protect you until they return.'

Imogene felt the wood slip from her hands. Two large tears rolled down her face and then wracking sobs followed as she comprehended Serena's words. She had experienced the love of the Great One – they were precious gifts, treasures to the Great One. For years they had pioneered and worked hard in their community. For years they had laid down everything in the hope of pleasing him and receiving his favour; and now it hit her with full force that he never required that of them. He did not need their service to make himself great and they did not need to earn his favour. All he wanted was for them to know his love and be happy.

Imogene sobbed out all the striving, all the pain, all the frustration and rejection that she felt as Serena held her, watching her heart heal a little more.

The two women sat at the fire talking about the Great One.

'Why don't more people want to follow him?' Imogene asked.

'Because they don't know how good he is. Stories have been told over time about the Great One and people think he is going to judge them and punish them for not following him. They don't realize that he loves them all and that nothing they do will ever keep his love from them. The Great One does not separate himself from anyone – his love and Lionsgate is open to all.

'Then why does the Dark Lord have so much control over people?'

'The Dark Lord loves to deceive people into believing that the Great One will punish those who don't listen. Fear is a great weapon and leads man into many false truths. Fear can never lead you to love the way you should.

'How sad,' Imogene said, yet in her heart she and Mac had done the same thing. They had subconsciously feared the Great One, believing they had to work hard to please him. She was determined they would never make that mistake twice.

The group alighted from the forest into the clearing where the two women were sitting. Mac held up the scroll triumphantly to Imogene. She was delighted to see them all, especially Ziah. She expected a sombre group to arrive back at the camp carrying his broken body. Seeing everyone together and in good spirits lifted her weary soul. The troubles were still not over – Mitchell was missing and Struan was feverish and had serious infection in his wounds, and yet despite all this Imogene felt peace and assurance that it would all be okay.

The Great One delved deep into the pocket of his robe and pulled out the vial of healing oil. He laughed at their look of confusion.

'Thank you for this but I didn't need it for Ziah as I'm the one who grants life. The fact that you were willing to lay down everything, even your son's life for me speaks of incredible love. This is true living – that we love in greater measure and that love would conquer all and usher in truth and life. Use the oil to heal your son's wounds.'

Imogene threw her arms around the old man. Words failed her. In the last few days they had learned more about this wonderful person than they had known in all the years they followed him. Somehow it felt right and okay to embrace him this way.

Ziah watched them, love reflected in his dark, beautiful eyes. He had been through pain and torment, and yet there was no evidence of the brutality he had endured. He watched Mac and Imogene gently apply the healing oil to Struan, the boy immediately responding to the miraculous potion. Struan sipped his broth hungrily while his parents explained all that had happened over the last few days. Ziah smiled – this family's world had been turned upside down – they had seen things they would never have dreamed possible. This was something they would walk in more and more in the future, secure in the knowledge they were loved by the entire kingdom of Lionsgate.

The morning began to dawn and the group readied themselves to move off. It was vital for them to leave this part of the Dark Lord's kingdom before it was discovered that Ziah and the Hamilton children were gone from the castle. The Great One chuckled to himself imagining Sephtis' confusion then fury as this was discovered. They gathered themselves together and began the journey back to Lionsgate. The trip was long, but triumphant as they made their way to the Glass Sea that would ultimately take them home to the majestic gates of the Great One's kingdom.

# CHAPTER 22

# RESOLUTION

*How few there are who have courage enough to own their faults, or
resolution enough to mend them*

— Benjamin Franklin

'OOH my head feels as though it is going to explode.'

Legion tried to clear his fuzzy head. It felt as though pins had been poked into his eye sockets and his thoughts were sluggish and muddled. What had happened last night? He remembered sweet Aislinn as she sipped her wine. He recalled vague memories of Ziah in his chamber, but that was impossible - the man was dead! Surely he couldn't have indulged in so much wine that he had passed out in front of the young girl? He felt a little embarrassed at the thought of this. He would go up to the tower and see her himself to apologize. He decided he wanted her no matter what and if he had to offer some comfort and privileges to her bratty brother and sister to achieve that, then he would. Once she was his queen, she would soon forget about them and he could send them away. After all, he had everything else, all he needed now was someone to share it with. The romantic dream formulated in his head making him smile.

A knock at the door had him groaning again as he held his aching head in his hands.

'Come in,' he called.

'Good morning Master. I trust you had a wonderful night's sleep?'

'What is it Falstaff? My head is splitting and I need some quiet.'

'The druids sent word about the keys Master. They have discovered the secret of them.'

Legion forgot all about his headache, leaning forward in anticipation.

'The keys can only be used if there is true love in a man's heart. Without it they are of no use.'

'Thank you Falstaff,' he replied. It was more important than ever for him to make Aislinn his queen now. It was the only way he would ever be able to use those keys!

His dream was short lived as there was shouting coming from the courtyard. What on earth was happening - why was there such a fiasco? *Didn't these people know he was in pain!*

Before long there was urgent knocking at his door.

'What now?' he called tentatively, holding his pounding head.

The door swung open revealing Morelock and Deception, each looking sickly green. They were nervous and frightened and each looked to the other hoping they would be the first to speak.

'What the devil's happening?' Legion asked, irritated.

'We have a problem Master,' Deception plucked up the courage to speak.

'Well what is it?'

'It seems Ziah's body was stolen during the night and replaced by some other drunken sod,' he nervously said.

'Is that all?' he mocked. 'What difference does it make? He was as dead as a doornail and won't be going anywhere. Maybe the vultures carried him off. Frankly, it is a blessing – saves us having to dispose his body.'

Legion's nonchalant attitude caught them by surprise. They had never seen him like this before. The truth was his thoughts were consumed by the sweet, innocent young girl, trapped up in the tower of his castle. He wanted to see her as soon as possible and this conversation was wasting his time.

'There's more,' Morelock muttered urgently. 'The Hamilton children are gone from the tower – they're nowhere to be seen.'

This news caught his attention, his face clouding over.

'Have you checked the kitchen?' he asked. 'Perhaps they are helping Cook with the clean-up.'

'We have checked everywhere Master. They are gone.'

Legion seemed momentarily confused. He had seen the young girl just the night before. She had shown such interest in him pouring him wine...

The realization that she had outwitted him dawned on him making him feel sick to his stomach. He had not passed out from too much wine - she had drugged him causing his blackout and this monstrous headache he was battling. Most of all, he was angry with himself for being deceived by her sweetness. *Where did she get the potion from?* Someone must have given it to her. He racked his brain trying to remember the foggy haze of the previous night's events. Again he recalled Ziah's voice in his chamber. Rushing over to his treasure box he silently cursed himself for his stupidity. Flinging the lid open, his trepidation was confirmed. The keys and scroll were gone and the emptiness mocked him.

The roar that emanated from his chamber reverberated around the stony walls of the castle and sent Falstaff, Morelock and Deception running in fear from his room. They all knew what this meant. He had been outwitted again by the Great One and this would make their Master angrier and meaner than ever before. This was not a good day for Griswold.

Legion paced backwards and forwards in his chamber. His affection for Aislinn was quickly replaced with deep hatred for her. He laughed sarcastically as he thought how she had outsmarted him at the game he was so adept at playing. How could he have been such a fool? This was Ziah's fault –he should have known the Great One would revive him. He had put her up to it – he was sure.

'You think you've won?' he shouted to the invisible Great One. 'I will never give up trying to defeat you,' he snarled. Now he had no hold over the Hamilton family either. The scroll and the keys were both lost to him. He was furious that he had lost the keys that held the power of life and death. They would truly have made him the most powerful person in the kingdom. He felt embarrassed that he had so little control over the circumstances. He would let his wizards and followers believe that Ziah's body had been stolen – if anyone found out that he was alive he would be the laughing stock of Griswold.

'This is just the beginning,' he vowed vehemently.

⌘

The atmosphere in Lionsgate was of extreme joy and celebration – the complete opposite of Griswold. The Great One's arrival with Ziah and Aedan at his side was announced by heralds sounding their trumpets. The sky displayed a rainbow so intense that it seemed to be alive and dancing with life of its own. Aislinn, Struan and Maddy marveled at the sight. Their parents had spoken of this place but they never imagined it to be so real and so incredible. There was real love here and a life force that surged. It was the most magical place they had ever been. They entered the castle through the large wooden gates. This place was so different to the Dark Lord's castle. A large banquet hall hosted an amazing feast set out before them and the children squealed in delight at the food choices.

'Eat and have your fill,' the Great One encouraged. 'You must all be very hungry.'

They ate the succulent fare, chatting together, feeling relaxed and secure for the first time in days. It was good to see Struan back to his old self – his appetite back.

'Here's the scroll, Great One.' Mac handed it to the old man. 'You're the one who should have it more than any of us.'

'Do you remember what you saw in the golden book regarding your life?'

Mac was momentarily confused, but then remembered how they had seen no record of their past mistakes, only good things they had done. He nodded.

The Great One saw understanding dawn on his face.

'I'm not keeping that scroll' he stated. 'I can't, because I chose to forget the mistakes you made. You need to do that too and that will not be possible if you keep that document.'

'Then we will destroy it,' Mac said emphatically.

⌘

Later that night when all was quiet and the children slept peacefully for the first time in days, Mac and Imogene pulled out the scroll. This was the written word of everything that was perceived by others about their service and lives. Their very integrity was laid out and challenged in this document. It was hard to believe that words on a piece of parchment could hold such power and change their lives so much, but it had.

'Do you want one last look before we destroy it?' he asked Imogene.

'No, what's past is past –there's no point dredging up hurtful memories again.'

Mac was relieved. He was not sure what he would have done if she had wanted to read through it. He knew it would anger and hurt them both afresh if they looked at it.

'So be it. This is the start of a new beginning for us. We must learn from the past, but never allow it to define who we are. Imogene we have been given a second chance at life – our destiny is in our hands and we can choose to do whatever we wish from this point on.

'Do you want to go back to doing what we did before,' she asked tentatively.

'I am grateful for the past and all we have experienced – yes, believe it or not even this sordid mess, because we learned so much about ourselves and the real nature of the Great One. There is no way I can ever go back to what we did before Imogene, even if the Prophecy declares it' because I think differently now and I can only do what my conscience and conviction allows.'

'Mac, I am so happy to hear you say that.'

They raised their goblets and drank agreement upon this statement, then took the scroll and threw it into the hearth to be consumed by the hungry flames. It was sealed and the beginning of a new future for them. The scroll caught fire, the words caught up in smoke, never to be seen again.

# CHAPTER 23

# GUILT

*People tend to dwell more on negative things than on good things.*
*So the mind then becomes obsessed with negative things, with judgments,*
*guilt and anxiety produced by thoughts about the future and so on*

— Eckhart Tolle

MITCHELL had not settled well in Morelock's home. He wanted his Mama and Linnie and he couldn't understand who this overbearing, suffocating woman was. He turned his face away in frustration and irritation when she tried to cuddle and kiss him. He was at a loss as to what had happened to his family and this was displayed through his demanding behaviour. He threw tantrums and yelled, holding his breath, turning deep purplish-blue in the face. This frightened Rozanne as she was not used to dealing with children and had little experience of how to resolve it. She was terrified that he would indeed stop breathing and succumb to the grip of the torment that seemed to be chasing him. She felt inadequate and frustrated and wondered how she could learn to be a good mother.

'Don't fret so much,' Morelock would say to his wife at the end of each day when she would besiege him with tears of frustration and failure. 'Give yourself some time to adjust. The wee one needs time too. This is all strange for him. Why don't you take him out a bit more during the day into the fresh country air, instead of keeping him cooped up in the house.'

The truth was that she was afraid to take him out in case she lost him or an accident befell him. Her lack of confidence only made the situation worse.

She decided then and there that she could not keep up this way of life. She needed help and she needed it fast.

⌘

'Mac, Imogene!' The voice called to them as they wandered in the beautiful grounds of Lionsgate. They had much to talk about and what life would hold for them now as a family. Mitchell was never far from their minds, and they knew the time would come to get him back, but they would need a solid plan for that to be a reality. Then they could make a fresh start anywhere they chose to go.

They glanced around looking for the voice. Regent was leaning against a tree eating the juicy, delicious fruit from it, wiping his mouth with his arm as the juice ran down his chin.

'Regent!'

He smiled, noting how time spent in this place had taken years off them and how freedom agreed with them. It was evident in the way they moved, spoke, but most of all in their eyes.

'I have news of Mitchell for you.'

Imogene caught her breath. She was afraid and yet hungry to know more.

'I've been watching over the little one as the Great One asked me to,' Regent continued.

Again Mac and Imogene realized how much the Great One cared for their family. He had never let Mitchell out of his sight, sending Regent to be there for him. They should have guessed Mitchell would be watched over.

'What can you tell us? Is he all right?' The questions tumbled out of Imogene's mouth one after another.

'He's healthy, but missing you. I have some other news you might be interested in.'

They waited, expectation written all over their faces.

'Rozanne, Morelock's wife is looking for a young girl to help her with the little lad. Rumours abound that she is struggling with his strong will,' Regent smiled.

Imogene and Mac smiled too. So she was discovering that even at his tender age, Mitchell could be quite a handful and stubborn on certain things.

'This could be an opportunity for someone to get close to Mitchell and get her trust so that he can be brought back home,' Regent suggested, letting the idea sink into their minds.

After Regent left they talked about the possibility of rescuing Mitchell. The information Regent had provided was useful but there was no way to implement it.

'You can't get the job looking after Mitchell, Imogene,' Mac said seeing the desperation in his wife's eyes.

'She's looking for a young girl to care for him, and although you are young and beautiful to me, they may not quite see you the same way I do,' he said, a mischievous look in his eyes.

She playfully punched him on the arm, feigning indignance.

'I know,' she said 'but it seems a wasted opportunity if we don't do something. Maybe Serena could help us – she's young and beautiful.'

They turned back to the castle, each with their own thoughts and plans mulling over in their minds.

'Mama, Papa,' Aislinn skipped down the marble stairs toward them, eager anticipation on her face.

'What's the hurry?' her father called.

'I've been speaking to Regent and he tells me that Morelock and his wife are looking for someone to help care for Mitchell and I thought....'

Her words were cut off by her father's emphatic tone.

'No Aislinn, you have done enough to help us get back the scroll and Ziah's keys. There is not a chance we will send you alone to that place. It's far too dangerous and I will not discuss this any further with you,' he said.

Her face fell in consternation and frustration.

'But Papa, why?'

'It was one thing to let you come with us when we went to get the scroll. There was a whole band of us to help you if you got into trouble. This time, there won't be that support. It's far too dangerous.'

'But I know I can do this,' she continued to press the issue. Her desire to see Mitchell safe and the guilt she felt dared her to cross the line.

'Enough!' Mac roared, losing his temper and then just as quickly feeling the shame of it. It was so out of order in this perfect place and it seemed as though everything cringed at his sharp tone.

'The matter is closed,' he said gently but equally firm.

Aislinn's tears ran freely down her face - she turned away from them and ran out of the castle into the beautiful day. She sat under a tree alongside the river and wept.

'Don't cry Aislinn. Lionsgate is not used to people crying – you might upset the balance of nature,' Regent teased. He had seen the exchange between daughter and parents and guessed what had transpired.

'They don't understand how I feel,' she confided in Regent. 'I'm the one who let them take Mitchell- I feel responsible for him.'

'It was never your fault Aislinn. There was no way you could have prevented that from happening. Believe it or not, they are protecting you because they love you and are fearful they will lose you too.'

'I know, but this could be the only chance we have to rescue him. I have to do it. Will you help me Regent?'

At dinner they all gathered in the great hall for another feast. The food, as always was sumptuous with flavours to tempt every tastebud.

'Where's Aislinn?' Imogene asked, noting her daughter absence.

'She's probably still sulking in her room,' her father replied. 'I will not give in on this matter – she needs to do as she is told.'

Imogene excused herself from the table to look for her daughter. Sulking was not tolerated in the Hamilton family. It was one value they wanted their children to learn.

'What is your concern?' the Great One asked noting Mac's agitation.

'Aislinn has this crazy plan in her head. She thinks she should get the job looking after Mitchell – Morelock and his wife are looking for someone young to fill the position. She thinks she might be able to get him back.'

'And why would you assume that it is a crazy plan?' the old man asked Mac soberly.

'Well she's too young, and it's too dangerous and …. it's just a crazy idea, that's all,' he said defensively, taken aback at the Great One's question.

'Perhaps the truth is that you are afraid you don't believe she's capable and you fear you will lose her,' he gently chided Mac.

Mac looked stupefied. Was the Great One really challenging his parenting ability?

He couldn't seriously expect him to let her go.

'Sometimes,' he continued unperturbed at Mac's disbelief, 'one has to let one's children go, to experience challenges and hardships that will grow and benefit not only themselves, but others in the family too. This is how they learn to make wise choices and become responsible adults. Your Aislinn has grown up a lot in the last few days looking after her siblings. I chose to forgive you and forget your mistakes, maybe you should choose to forgive her and forget her mistakes. She feels responsible for the little lad being taken away and in her mind she needs to rectify that.'

'But it isn't her fault,' Mac said.

'Yes, and some of what happened to you and your family wasn't your fault either, but I chose to allow you the opportunity to get back the scroll that was stolen from you and because of it, you are now able to move on with your life and start anew,' The Great One pointed out.

Understanding filled Mac's face. Of course he understood how that felt. It had felt good taking that scroll back and having the power to decide what to do with it. In fact, it had made all the difference in healing their hearts. Even though they didn't blame Aislinn for Mitchell's disappearance she was carrying guilt for it and to move on she needed to do this. He would talk to Imogene and convince her that the plan may yet work.

She came rushing into the hall, worry etched on her face.

'Aislinn's gone,' she cried holding up the note she had found in place of her daughter.

The note was short and scribbled as though she were in a hurry.

*Forgive me for disobeying you both. I love you, but I love Mitchell too and this may be the only way to get him back. Don't worry about me, Regent is with me and will send news regularly of our progress. I hope you don't mind, but I have taken the glasses and the truth ring with me.*

*All my love, Aislinn.*

Mac smiled.

'Well I guess that is that and there is no more we can do.'

Imogene looked at her husband as though he were mad. She could not believe he was going to do nothing and she stormed out of the hall.

'Looks like you might be sleeping on the chaise tonight,' the Great One chuckled.

⌘

Aislinn and Regent crossed the Glass Sea and travelled back toward Griswold. Morelock and his wife lived in a humble cottage on the Dark Lord's estate and Aislinn knew she would have to be careful that no one recognize her, as it could jeopardize the entire mission. She had covered her curly hair with a scarf. Her attire was neither opulent nor that of a peasant as she did not want to attract unnecessary attention to herself. Regent was disguised as a weary traveller passing through with her. As they came to the cottages and the humble inn in the little village they made an effort to neaten themselves and dust their clothing. They were tired and their feet ached from the journey.

It was dark and dreary inside the little inn. The only air of homeliness that it had was the crackling fire in the hearth and the wafting smell of soup in the air. It was almost empty as the hour was not late enough for the serious revellers to arrive.

A middle-aged woman who looked tired was behind the counter polishing silver goblets. A cat stretched on an old armchair and a young girl stoked the fire sending embers into the air.

'Good afternoon Madam,' Regent said politely bowing his head momentarily. 'The young mistress and I have been on the road many days and we are very weary,' he said indicating Aislinn. 'Her father is a merchant and often away and her poor mother has departed this world. My wife I are all that she has and her father has entrusted her to our care while he is away,' he continued noticing the curiosity in the woman's eyes.

One did not often see a young fair skinned girl with a man whose skin was as dark as the night.

'Where is your wife?' the older woman asked, mistrust in her eyes.

'Well that's the problem,' said Regent. 'She has taken ill with fever and a rash, so I needed to get the young one out of our home till she recovers. My master would never forgive me if his daughter became ill.'

'Where are you taking her?' the woman questioned.

'I have nowhere to take her, but I was wondering if she could take a room here at the inn? She could help with some chores, just till things get back to normal,' he asked.

'We have no room here,' the woman insisted. She had no desire to be responsible for a young girl. What if she had caught the fever and infected her entire inn?

'However there is a young woman looking for help with her wee one in the village. Perhaps she could help you in return for the young lass helping her,' she added.

'Where do we find her?'

They could hear Mitchell throwing a tantrum as they arrived outside the little house. Regent cautioned Aislinn with his eyes not to get emotional – this was important or their cover would be blown. He knocked loudly on the door.

A dishevelled, fraught looking woman opened the door, desperation in her eyes and face.

'Yes,' she spat out rudely to them. 'What do you want? I'm rather busy.'

Regent explained their plight and how they could help one another. This was music to Rozanne's ears– she was at the end of her tether with her situation. She could not control this little boy any longer. She flung the door open wide and gratefully invited them in. To her surprise, Mitchell stopped crying the instant Aislinn walked into the room. He looked at her through tearful eyes, his trembling lip turning up into a little smile. He toddled over to her and put his hands out looking for a cuddle, which she duly gave to him.

Rozanne was astounded.

'It seems the young lad is taken with you Miss,' she said amazed. 'Would you be willing to stay awhile and help me with him? We'll feed you well and give you a bed to sleep in, until you are able to return to your father.'

Aislinn nodded her head demurely, but inside she was jumping up and down in excitement. Their plan had worked.

'What do want our little Mitch to call you,' she asked.

'Linnie,' Aislinn said. She knew that Mitchell would use it. She had been terrified that he would call her by name when he first saw her. The fact that he had not, was a miracle and she could use her nickname safely now. No one would associate Linnie with Aislinn.

'Linnie,' Mitchell echoed and they all laughed.

Regent made sure that Aislinn was settled in and then said his goodbyes.

'I will never be far from you. Sometimes you will not see me he said, but know that I am near – you are not alone,' he reassured her.

'I hope my parents forgive me for this.'

'They will,' he said. 'They are learning in all of this too Aislinn. Now, make sure you use the glasses and ring when you need to. If you're in trouble, leave this red ribbon tied to the window latch in your room. If I see it I'll know you need help.'

They hugged one another and then Regent left the little cottage.

Aislinn had some concerns that Morelock would recognize her. She had been cleaning the Dark Lord's chambers a couple of times when he had met with the Dark Lord. She hoped that he had not paid her much attention and that his memory would be foggy on the details of those meetings. She had never directly spoken to him and she hoped this would be in her favour – still it was a risk she would have to take. She spent the rest of the day cuddling Mitchell and playing with him. She helped to feed him and bathe him and she felt happy protecting him again. She had to continually remind herself to call him Mitch and not Mitchell as it would arouse suspicion if she used his full name.

Dusk began to descend and Rozanne lit the little fire to cook a thick beef stew. It smelled delicious and Aislinn looked forward to dinner. It wouldn't be quite as delicious as the food they had eaten in Lionsgate, but it would be wholesome, tasty and filling. Aislinn heard the horse outside the cottage and she tensed her shoulders in anticipation. This was the moment of truth. Morelock would either recognize her or she would be safe. This was the riskiest part of the whole plan and she had no way of knowing how it would end. She sent up a prayer to the Great One and readied herself for the encounter. Morelock entered the cottage looking tired and distracted. His wife embraced him and helped him remove his coat. She gave him no opportunity to speak as she chatted away animatedly of the day's events.

'We have a guest with us for a while,' she said waving at Aislinn. 'This young lady is the girl I've selected to help me with Mitch. They get along so well and already today he has been more settled and of a happier disposition.'

Morelock glanced briefly at Aislinn, a flicker of recognition in his eyes, but then it was gone just as fast.

'Pleased to meet you miss,' he greeted her. 'Anyone who helps Rozanne is a friend of mine – I hope you will be comfortable here.'

'Thank you sir,' she replied, relief flooding her heart. For just a moment she thought he had placed her and she was terrified.

'Dinner's ready,' Rozanne called to them both.

⌘

Later that night, as she lay in bed, she could hear Morelock and Rozanne moving around their living room, the paper-thin walls hardly concealing their conversation.

'It's been a tough few days at the castle,' he muttered to his wife. 'I don't know how much longer we can tolerate the Dark Lord's wrath and bad temper. Ever since the Great One's son and the Hamilton children disappeared, he has been impossible. He hates to lose and this has been a bitter pill for him to swallow. He takes it out on us continually.'

'Come sit by the fire. I'll get you a little wine to help you relax,' she coaxed. 'The things you do for that man – he doesn't know how lucky he is to have someone as loyal as you working for him.'

'Yes, and now we are forever indebted to him since he's given us the little one as our own. I have no choice but to remain loyal if we want to keep Mitch.'

The gift of the child came at a great price – they were not even aware how much they had sold themselves to the Dark Lord and the burden it would become. This was one gift that would haunt them in the days to come.

⌘

Aislinn lay in her bed looking out the little window at the starry sky. Guilt had made her impulsive in her decision to find Mitchell. She had to admit that she was afraid. She was afraid of being found out by the Dark Lord, but mostly of disappointing and failing her parents. What if she could not succeed at this mission? She hoped her parents would forgive her for running off but there was no other plan. This was their only hope of getting Mitchell back. She had not protected him and now it was her responsibility to get him back. She could not fail – it was not an option!

'Help me Great One,' she whispered to the night sky. 'Please give me an opportunity to make this right. Give me favour in this household.'

She watched as a shooting star whizzed across the inky black night and she smiled feeling that he had heard her plea. It would be all right - it had to be.

⌘

The Great One smiled – this girl had more courage than she knew. She would learn much about herself on this journey and it would make her stronger. She may feel guilty about not protecting Mitchell right now but this would soon be ancient history. Aislinn Hamilton had a great future in store for her. Of that he had no doubt.

# CHAPTER 24
## PATIENCE

*Patience is bitter, but its fruit is sweet*

— Aristotle

LEGION'S mood did not improve as the days following Aislinn's betrayal passed. He felt a mixture of fury, hopelessness, frustration and powerlessness at being defeated by the Great One and that slip of a girl again. He could not understand how his foolproof plan had gone wrong - it had seemed so perfect. He had nothing left to bargain with – no keys, no scroll, no Ziah and no Hamilton children. What was he going to do?

'There must be something I can use as a bargaining chip,' he muttered to himself.

A voice spoke from the doorway of his chamber. 'What about the little one Master?'

Legion looked up surprised to see a little goblin eavesdropping.

'Who are you?' he asked.

'Gossip,' he said, smiling at the Dark Lord, mischief in his eyes. 'I've been in the village and I have heard that one of your wizards has acquired a new child in the family – a gift from you I believe?'

'Yes, what is your point Gossip?' Legion asked, irritation creeping into his voice.

'Well Master, isn't the child a Hamilton?'

'Well what of it?' he snapped, becoming incensed at this annoying little creature.

'If you take the child back and use him to bargain with the Great One, you could get whatever you wanted,' he replied.

'Ah yes I see what you mean,' Legion said thoughtfully.

'There is just one problem with that idea. Morelock is one of my up and coming wizards with great talent and he has the ability to do great things for me. If I take away his heart's desire then I will not only alienate and anger him, I will lose out on two great wizards. I see the young Mitchell Hamilton becoming well trained in the art of magic – sometimes one has to delay instant gratification for the greater picture to be fulfilled. It will be equally painful for the Great One to see Mitchell Hamilton fighting for the dark side.'

The thought of that made him smile maliciously. Yes, he would have to be very patient – this could take years to work out in his favour, but he had waited a long time for the taste of victory and he was quite happy to wait for as long as it took. Yes, this was the solution and it would take time, but the victory would be so sweet when it came!

⌘

Regent checked in daily at the cottage. He was careful never to be seen, but he had to make certain that the red ribbon was not hanging from the window latch. Each day he was relieved to find the latch free of the ribbon. It was all working out splendidly – Aislinn was able to be with Mitchell and to help care for him. As yet, she still did not have the freedom to take him outdoors unaccompanied by

Rozanne, but she was biding her time, waiting for the young woman to trust her implicitly. She was both grateful for the time with Mitchell but also apprehensive at being discovered and eager to get back to her family. She looked forward to the time they would be reunited and would be able to make a new life for themselves, far away from Griswold.

As she helped to cook the dinner and ready Mitchell for his evening bath, she chatted to Rozanne.

'We have a guest coming for dinner tonight,' Rozanne said suddenly.

Aislinn felt alarmed and a little fearful.

'I'll put Mitch to bed for you and retire early then,' she said as nonchalantly as she could. 'That will give you time with your guest,' she added.

'Nonsense child, you are part of the family now. You will stay up and meet our guest.' Rozanne said adamantly and the matter was settled.

Aislinn prayed that it was someone who hadn't met her. She excused herself for a while and headed to her bedroom. She had an uneasy feeling about dinner tonight and she wanted to be ready if it all came tumbling down. She pulled out the red ribbon and tied it in a bow, ready to slip onto the latch if need be.

Then she made her way back to the kitchen.

Wizard Falstaff knocked at the door of the little cottage. He did not often come to Morelock's home – most of their dealings were at the Dark Lord's castle when they were working on spells and potions and poring over new books that would teach them amazing new wizardry skills. Deep down he was jealous of Morelock. The young man certainly had a gift for wizardry and as his favour with the Dark Lord increased, so did Falstaff's unease that his days as the chief wizard may be coming to a swift end. Nonetheless, Morelock had invited him for dinner – he wanted him to meet Mitch and to talk over a few new spell ideas that he had. Falstaff had decided to come, as he felt more secure keeping Morelock close by, knowing what the young man was up to.

Rozanne opened the door and welcomed him in.

'Good evening Wizard Falstaff. Come in and warm yourself by the fire,' she invited. 'I will get you some wine.'

'Thank you,' he mumbled looking around the little cottage with keen interest.

It was a humble little dwelling but the love and attention to detail made it homely and comfortable.

He noticed Aislinn sitting on the floor, little Mitch curled up in her lap. Aislinn kept her head bent down over the little boy. The hair on her neck prickled in fear and dread. She had recognized Falstaff's voice as he greeted Rozanne. Many times she had been in the Dark Lord's chamber when Falstaff had come to see him. Although they had never spoken, she was certain he had seen her.

Again she sent up a prayer to the Great One.

'This must be the new addition to the family?' Wizard Falstaff asked moving over to where Aislinn was sitting.

'Yes,' Rozanne answered, 'and this is Linnie our helper. She's helping me with Mitch for a while until her father returns from trading and what a godsend she has been. '

He glanced at Aislinn and sensed something very familiar about her. What was it? He could not quite put his finger on it, and it bothered him immensely. Never mind, it would come to him – he was sure.

'Good evening,' Aislinn said politely. She wished the evening were over. She would have to be very careful not to arouse his suspicions. She had pulled her hair back hoping that her appearance would be a little different to when she was a prisoner in the Dark Lord's castle. Falstaff smiled at her then turned to receive the wine goblet Rozanne held out to him. The dinner went off very well and eventually Falstaff made his excuses of too much wine and a full belly to retire for the evening.

Aislinn heaved a sigh of relief as she flopped down on her bed. It had been a stressful evening but she was sure everything would be okay now. He had not indicated that he recognized her. She closed her eyes, thanked the Great One and drifted off into a peaceful sleep.

Wizard Falstaff was not as fortunate. The combination of too much wine and too much food left him tossing and turning in a dream filled state that was half awake and half asleep. His mind grappled with the face of a sweet young girl while trying to grasp at sleep. His memory was trying to place that face. When he did sleep he dreamed of the Dark Lord and trying to win his favour, intermingled with Morelock being elected as the next chief wizard. In his dream the Master promoted Morelock while he was left in a dark corner of the chamber watching on. Morelock and the other wizards looked at him, contempt on their faces and he felt small and afraid. Then he noticed someone else looking on – a young girl in the Dark Lord's chamber. She was cleaning his things and when his eyes met hers, he knew who she was – she was Aislinn Hamilton – the same young girl living in Morelock's home!

## CHAPTER 25

# REVELATION

*The revelation of thought takes men out of servitude into freedom*
— Ralph Waldo Emerson

WIZARD Falstaff was restless but excited as well. He had the trump card up his sleeve and he planned to use it for his own benefit. He had woken from his fitful sleep with the realization that Aislinn Hamilton was living right here in the village under the Dark Lord's nose. Linnie and Aislinn were one and the same! He wondered if Morelock was aware of it. Somehow he didn't think so and he didn't really care as he smiled to himself. Oh how fortune had smiled upon him today. The Master would be very pleased with his discovery and may even reward him for it.

He knocked on Legion's chamber door and waited to be ushered in.

'What is it Falstaff?' Legion asked glancing up from his breakfast tray.

'Good morning Master. I have some good news for you.'

'I could certainly use good news Falstaff. What is it?'

'I had dinner at Morelock's home last night and made a startling discovery,' he continued, seeing curiosity in the Master's eyes. 'They have young lass helping them with the little Hamilton boy, and I thought I recognized her, but I couldn't place her all evening. Then it came to me during the night. I had seen her before – right here in your chamber Master.'

'Well, what of it? I have a number of young chambermaids that come in here to clean and tidy. Perhaps Morelock asked one of them to help his wife in her spare time. I don't have a problem with that Falstaff. What is this really about? Why are you trying to get Morelock into trouble – are you perhaps jealous of him?'

Falstaff flushed deep crimson at the truth of these words, but he continued nevertheless.

'No Master, I'm not trying to get Morelock into trouble. In fact I don't think he knows who she really is,' he ventured.

'I'm not following you Falstaff – you're speaking in riddles,' Legion said annoyed. 'Could you please just get it out, whatever it is.'

'It's the Hamilton girl, Master – Aislinn. She's the one caring for her little brother.'

Legion went rigid. His arm stopped in mid-air, the spoon that held his porridge dripping the sticky mess back into the bowl. His icy demeanour spoke volumes and Falstaff felt fear tickle him gently like a feather. Had he gone too far?

'Are you sure about this Falstaff?' he asked coldly.

'Yes Master, I am certain.'

'Leave me, I need to think.'

Morelock was unaware of the drama unfolding. He arrived at the castle in a good mood – his wife was content, their home had turned into a peaceful place again with the help of Linnie there. He pottered away in his spell chamber adjusting spells in his book and concocting new spells, humming away to himself. His solitude was interrupted by a goblin with a cheeky face.

'The Master wants you in his chamber now.' The goblin had a smirk on his face.

Morelock had no idea what the Dark Lord wanted, but one didn't keep him waiting when he summoned. He quickly removed the concoction from the heat and stored away his spell book safely in the chest. It wouldn't do to have others sneaking a look at the spells he was working on.

'Come in Morelock,' Legion said slowly in answer to his knock on the door. He needed to keep his temper in check to verify Falstaff's accusations. He found it hard to believe that Morelock would deliberately deceive him – especially after seeing how Ziah was executed – traitors were dealt with severely in Griswold and Morelock knew that. Besides the young wizard and his wife had been so elated at receiving the Hamilton boy – surely that alone would keep them loyal to his service forever. They knew the risk of crossing him would mean losing the little boy and crushing their dreams of having a family of their own ever again.

'What can I do for you Master?'

'I believe you have found someone to help with your new young son?' he asked.

'Yes Master. Rozanne found a young girl to help her. She's waiting for her father to return from trading. We are providing a bed and meals in return for her help with the young lad. It has been a godsend I might add.'

'And how does she get along with the little man?' he asked feigning interest. 'I seem to remember he was quite strong willed?'

'Yes he is, but for some reason he really has become attached to her and it is working very well, thank you

Master,' he replied, pleased that the Master was interested in his family's welfare. It seemed out of character for the Dark Lord to concern himself with others welfare and Morelock was a little confused as to where this conversation was going. Perhaps he was in a better mood after his defeat and things would be different around the castle. Morelock hoped so.

The next question shattered any illusions he may have had.

'Could he be so attached to her because she is his sister?' he asked, studying Morelock's face for his reaction to the question.

Morelock cocked his head to one side as though he had heard incorrectly. He looked confounded at what the Master was implying. It was written all over his face and the Dark Lord was convinced that he did not know who the young girl was.

'I'm afraid I don't know what you mean Master.'

'The young girl in your home is none other than Aislinn Hamilton posing as someone else. She has deceived you and Rozanne, probably in the hope of stealing the young boy back. Falstaff has confirmed her identity.'

Morelock looked shocked and bewildered.

'I...I... I don't know what to say Master. I had no idea! I did not deal with her when she was in the castle and so I guess it never entered my head it could be her.'

Cold dread hit Morelock. His Master may well kill him for this mistake if he did not believe his story.

'Relax Morelock, I believe you – I know you always see the best in people – that is actually what I like about you. However we need to make this right and unfortunately it will require you to make a choice. You can keep the little

Hamilton boy in return for his sister, or you can choose to keep the girl in your home and I will take the little boy back. One thing is certain though. You may not keep them both. What's it to be?'

Morelock felt the blood drain from his face. They could not lose Mitch – it would devastate Rozanne and his dreams of a son and heir to follow in his footsteps would be shattered. He was angry at how Falstaff had gone over his head straight to the Master. He could have told Morelock what he had discovered but it was clear now to him that Falstaff only had his own interests at heart. He did not want to think about the fate of the girl, even though he should be angry at her deception. He knew the Dark Lord had been played so cunningly by Aislinn and that he would show no mercy to her, but he was left with no choice in the matter – her or Mitch – there was no choice.

⌘

Aislinn saw Morelock returning home through the window of the cottage. It was unusual for him to be home in the middle of the day. She saw his face, fearful and angry, and knew that something was wrong. Her heart lurched in her chest, a knot forming in her stomach.

'Rozanne, we need to talk now,' he barked at his wife as he marched through the door. The alarm on her face was visible as she jumped to her feet and followed him to their room. Aislinn scooped up Mitch and carried him to her room. *Should she flee with the child now while they were busy?* She strained to hear what was being spoken in the next room. They were talking in hushed, urgent voices. She caught the words 'Dark Lord knows' and 'Falstaff' and 'Hamilton girl'. It didn't take long for her to figure out that she had been discovered. So Falstaff had recognized her after all. Fear gripped her so intensely that she felt as though she would vomit. Quickly, with shaking hands she tied the red ribbon onto the window latch praying that Regent would see it soon.

That was all she had time for as she noticed four horsemen arriving at the cottage, Falstaff at the front, a victorious smirk on his face. There was no time to flee with Mitchell after all.

Once again, her life was being ripped from her control. She watched Mitchell crying as she was bound and scooped up onto the horse of the cloaked man. He had started this nightmare for their family and again he was the one the Dark Lord had called upon to sever her freedom. She still felt that flicker of recognition but she could not place him. Her feeling of loathing showed in her brilliant blue eyes. He looked away unable to hold her gaze.

Their arrival at the castle caused some speculation and curious faces peered at Aislinn. Some had pity in their eyes and others had malice and glee. All knew she would receive no mercy from the Dark Lord. The one thing he despised more than anything was being made a fool of and she certainly had done that.

She was dragged from the courtyard and thrown into the very same dungeon that Ziah had been in. She cowered in the corner away from the vermin that shared her cell.

⌘

Legion smiled. He had decided not to see her yet. His fury bubbled deep in his evil heart and he did not want his emotion to dictate his decisions. He wanted to think carefully about how to best utilize her capture. As much as he wanted to see her die a slow and painful death, he needed to work out how this could gain him power and victory. He determined not to act hastily in his anger – that had gotten him in trouble before. How could she help him to overcome the Great One? It was no use trying to kill Ziah again – that was impossible when the Great One just raised him to life. No, he had to find a way to kill the old man himself. If he could remove him then his powers would be obsolete. There must be a way. In the meantime he had a bargaining chip again.

## CHAPTER 26
## TRUST

*Love all, trust a few, do wrong to none*
— William Shakespeare, All's Well That Ends Well

REGENT looked up at the window, noticing the red ribbon fluttering in the breeze. He had hoped it would not come to this and a dreadful feeling settled in the pit of his stomach. He turned away and made his way back to Lionsgate. This was not good news – Mac and Imogene would not receive it well.

Mac and Imogene looked gravely concerned as Regent told them of Aislinn's capture and the Dark Lord's discovery. They feared for her life and of ever seeing her again. Ziah was equally distressed. He felt responsible in some way and headed out into the garden to think.

As he walked, his father joined him and wrapped his arm around his son.

'How will we rescue her father?' he asked? 'If I have to go through all that torture again even just for her, I can do it,' he declared passionately.

His Father smiled, pride and overwhelming love in his eyes.

'No Ziah, it is not necessary for you to die again or to pay any price,' he said gently.

'Everything was accomplished when you returned to us. Sephtis knows that you have defeated death and that he will not achieve victory that way.'

But how do we help Aislinn?' Ziah asked urgently.

'You have the keys of life and death and you know how they can be used,' the Great One continued. 'Aislinn knows she can trust us – she will call for those keys and when she does, she will have the power that comes from them and from the Key Keeper.'

'What if she doesn't call for them father?'

'She will. Have a little faith son. She knows how to trust – it won't let her down.'

'Is there some way we can show her what to do?'

'There are always ways to speak to our people – they need to understand what they experience and interpret it - we can speak to Aislinn through her dreams Ziah. I will help her to unlock the mystery – if she believes it, she has the ability to receive it.'

⌘

Aislinn sat in the dungeon, thinking over all that had happened to their family in just a few short weeks. It seemed unbelievable to think that only seventeen days ago they were carefree and living each day the same as any other. Who could conceive that life could change so radically in one moment and that all one's values, beliefs and mindsets could be challenged with the twinkling of an eye?

'What are you thinking so deeply about?' a voice echoed around the hollow dungeon. Aislinn looked up startled and then smiled seeing Ryder leaning against the cold stone wall.

'Ryder, it's good to see you.' She half laughed and half sobbed in relief.

'Well, I did say I would protect you, and you do seem to get yourself into some pretty awful situations young lady,' he said humorously.

Aislinn smiled, her face flushing crimson. She felt a little foolish for not thinking through her actions. She had followed her heart and had not used wisdom in planning Mitchell's rescue but worst of all she had been independent in her actions. She could not blame Regent – it was his job to protect her and he had done it well. She should have sought counsel from Ziah or the Great One before she disappeared.

'How am I going to get out of here Ryder?' she asked.

'You'll figure it out Aislinn, and when you do, you will be free in more ways than one. I must go now, but remember I am always close by.'

Aislinn was a little confused. Ryder was talking in riddles and she had no idea what he meant. How was she going to figure it out? She had no idea how to escape this awful place. She was hoping he would give her a solution.

She felt frustrated and fearful and a lonely tear rolled down her cheek. She brushed it away angrily. The last thing she needed now was a riddle to solve. She knew he was close by yet she felt so alone. She thought of Ziah and how he must have felt when he was locked in this place. Had he felt lonely and helpless too?

She shook herself slightly. She could not allow her courage to desert her now. Whatever happened, she needed to be brave and face the consequences of her actions. Self-pity was a destroying thing. It would lead to despair which would lead to further self-pity. It was a never-ending cycle and she determined in her heart not to go there.

'Great One, Ziah,' she quietly called. 'Can you hear me?'

The walls remained eerily silent and the gloomy dungeon stared back at her coldly.

The Great One and Ziah had indeed heard Aislinn. They saw her lonely figure in the cavernous dungeon through the Mirror of Time. Ziah paced, up and down, like a prowling lion, his brow creased in concern. *When would she call for the keys? Would she know what to do and what would happen if she didn't call for them?* He didn't want to think about it. He felt like he was waiting in anticipation and wished he could just go to her, but he knew the keys only worked if people called for them.

Mac and Imogene retreated to their room as the news of Aislinn's capture had been a devastating blow to them. Mac kept seeing Ziah's broken and tortured body and the thought of Aislinn suffering the same fate made him feel sick and afraid. Imogene sat staring into space – she had shut herself away to prevent her heart from breaking any more. When would this nightmare end?

⌘

Legion smiled to himself. He had Aislinn back in his castle and Morelock had proved his allegiance to him by choosing to hand over the girl. He had known it was a wise move to give the young boy to the young wizard and his wife. What Morelock hadn't realized yet was that it was a strategic move on his part to keep him bound forever. The young man would always feel indebted and that was the way he intended to keep it. Things were working out rather nicely after all.

⌘

'What are you doing Rozanne?' Morelock shrieked.

His wife ignored him as she loaded the little boy into the wagon and climbed up next to him. He reached out and grabbed her arm, panic knotting his stomach into a ball.

He was still trying to get his head around the young girl being forcefully removed from his home. His conscience was accusing him constantly as Rozanne had yelled at him to stop them, to do something. He had just stood by and allowed Cillian to take her. Rozanne didn't understand but she would – he would make sure of it.

'Where are you going Roz?'

'I don't care anymore about the Dark Lord's approval or tiptoeing around him. Sometimes things are glaringly wrong and need to be righted,' she said stubbornly shaking his arm off.

'Keep your voice down Roz,' Morelock glanced nervously about him. 'The walls have ears in Griswold - if this gets back to the Dark Lord, both of us will be strung up for the birds to peck. Let's go inside and discuss this rationally. I will explain it all to you.'

His sweet, imploring tone had no effect on her steely resolve.

'There's nothing to explain. You did nothing when they took that girl – I don't know you anymore. You are the one who needs to decide,' she continued, fierce determination in her voice, 'it's him or it's me. You have such talent and are so gifted and he overlooks you all the time. He keeps you on a string and now with Mitch as the pawn he has you right where he wants. Well no more! This little boy is going back to his parents and if the Great One will have us, I think we should seek his counsel and help. I will not have that girl's death on my conscience.'

Morelock paled at her suggestion. It was not the idea of returning Mitch that did it. Firstly, he imagined the Dark Lord's fury if he found out what they were planning and then he imagined what the Great One would do to them if they went to him. They had been part of killing his son – not directly of course, but he was still working for the Dark Lord. However he knew that she was speaking the truth. Aislinn would not receive a pardon the second time around – she would certainly be killed for her treachery. Why did everyone feel the need to make him choose?

The fear in his eyes was not lost on his wife. She too felt caught between the Dark Lord and the Great One and each scenario was equally terrifying, but somehow facing the Great One seemed less daunting. She had heard stories in Griswold of the Great One's goodness and His marvellous sense of humour. Those qualities she knew did not exist in the Dark Lord. She sincerely hoped that the stories she had heard were true. The thing she was most afraid of though, was losing her husband – already he was turning a blind eye to evil – the Dark Lord was changing his character. If they did not get away from here he would be lost to her forever.

'Morelock, I know you are afraid. Aren't you tired of looking over your shoulder every five minutes? We will never be free if we stay here. Please come with me. I need you,' she pleaded.

⌘

Aislinn closed her eyes and drifted into a restless sleep. She was tired as the stress of the last few hours caught up with her. Her dreams were vivid and muddled. They were filled with mocking eyes and evil creatures closing in around her. She felt panic and desperation as she tried to escape their rancid breath and their sharp claws scratching at her garments. In her dreamy haze she saw a door that would provide escape. She ran toward it, hearing footsteps hounding her. The beating of her heart was deafening – time was running out, she would be caught and torn to shreds. She clawed the door handle, pulling with all her might but it would not budge. She noticed a key hole but there was no key.

'I need a key, I need a key,' she screamed. 'Where is it?'

'Everything is possible Aislinn if you only believe.' Regent floated through her dreams, his words echoing.

The last thing she saw, before jolting awake, was a silhouette of a man holding keys in his hands as she stretched out her arm trying to reach for them.

Sweat ran off her brow. The dream was so vivid and her heart raced in fear, her body trembling. It left her shaken and she wondered what it meant. Papa always said that dreams were your imagination's way of communicating things. He said it was also the way the Great One sometimes communicated with you. Did the dream mean something and if so, what was the message? She didn't like the feeling of being hunted in her dream, her way of escape blocked. It was frightening. She mulled it over and over in her mind, seeking answers. The man with the keys seemed familiar and yet she couldn't place him. Perhaps it would come to her.

⌘

Rozanne and Morelock continued to argue in angry, whispered tones. There was no way Rozanne was going to change her mind and Morelock knew it was futile trying to convince her otherwise. This woman could be as stubborn as a mule when she wanted to be. Mitchell looked at them, uncertain, his bottom lip quivering at their angry raised voices, his big eyes beginning to fill with tears.

'I don't want a child this way,' she blurted out eventually. 'It feels as though we have him illegitimately and I will always feel as though his sister's blood will be on our hands. I can't live this way anymore. As much as I love you Morelock, I have to do what I feel in my heart. If I don't, it will destroy me. I'll understand if you can't come with me.'

Morelock frowned. He had not really thought how this turn of events would affect her. All he had wanted was to make her happy – to give her the child she so longed for. Seems he had failed once again in that department.

'What do you suppose we do Rozanne? Where would we go? You're not thinking clearly. We can't go to the Great One.'

He needed to think without her nagging – he longed for the quiet of his spell chamber.

'Roz, I need to think about this awhile. I'm already late for work. We'll talk about this later. Please don't leave until I come home. Promise me...' he said gathering up his cloak and heading for the door.

'Don't think you can escape. I won't let this go,' she warned. 'You'll have to face reality sometime,' she yelled at his receding back. 'I won't wait much longer!'

Morelock rode his faithful old steed down the road, the clip-clopping of its hooves like a steady metronome. His mind was far off as he thought through all their options and the repercussions should they flee Griswold. The Dark Lord would hunt them – of that he was certain. That's if the Great One didn't finish them off first. He did not see the shaft of light that exploded from the sky, so deep in thought was he. His horse reared in fright and threw him onto his back, galloping off leaving the startled man in the dust. As he lay there, winded, he tried to make sense of the dazzling light that blinded him. He covered his eyes with his arm, his heart beating fearfully in his chest. Had one of the Dark Lord's goblins somehow overheard his and Rozanne's conversation?

'Who are you?' he asked the radiant light. He didn't feel as confident as his voice sounded. 'What do you want?'

'Morelock, why are you running from the truth? You are being blind to what is going on around you.'

'No I'm not,' Morelock defended.

As the words escaped his lips so his eyes clouded over – glassy and unseeing.

'I can't see – I can't see... what have you done to me?'

He felt the ground around him, panic engulfing him, suffocating him. Fear gripped his heart.

'What do you want from me?' he shrieked feeling completely vulnerable now.

'I want you to see what I see in you. You have a gift and how you choose to use it will determine the path you take in this life. Seems to me you have taken the road of fear and bondage. Do you want to spend the rest of your days in debt to someone like the Dark Lord?'

The voice was gentle – not mocking or harsh and he realized that this was not someone sent by the Dark Lord. Relief flooded him momentarily.

'I don't know how to escape from him. I am afraid to stay but I am equally afraid to go. What should I do?' he asked dropping his head in his hands.

'Take Rozanne and the child and go to Lionsgate to the Great One – he will help you.'

'Why would he help me? I was there when they killed his son. I did nothing to help him – I just looked away and justified his death in my mind and now I have done the same with Aislinn Hamilton – I turned a blind eye.'

The irony of his statement was not lost on him.

'It's okay Morelock. The Great One sees more than appearances – he sees right into your heart and it is not as evil as you believe. Everyone is redeemable.'

The voice let out a shrill whistle that startled Morelock and soon he heard horse hooves approaching.

'I will help you onto your horse – he will take you back home. When you get home and tell Rozanne that you are going, your sight will return. Leave as soon as you can. Follow the emerald dove – it will take you safely to Lionsgate.'

'Who are you?' he asked again.

'Ziah.'

Morelock gasped, his colour fading.

'That's not possible –Ziah's dead. I saw his body myself.'

'And yet you have just spoken to me Morelock. The Dark Lord is not as powerful as he wants you to believe. Now go – time is moving on and you need to escape before someone comes looking for you.'

The horse stood patiently as Ziah helped the young man into the saddle.

'Why are you helping me? I don't understand! You could just kill me right now.'

'Because love never fails – as you will discover Morelock. I'm asking you to trust me. Can you do that?

He nodded. He was out of choices.

'Take him home boy,' Ziah whispered to the horse.

Rozanne heard the horse coming up the path. She had not expected Morelock back so soon. Maybe he had come to his senses after all, or maybe something bad had happened. She opened the door tentatively and stepped out into the sunshine, squinting her eyes against the glare.

'You're home already,' she stated. She noticed his blank eyes and how he fumbled with the reins.

'Morelock,' she cried alarmed, 'what's happened? What has the Dark Lord done to you?'

'It's okay Rozanne, I'm fine. This is not the work of the Dark Lord but the Great One's way of helping me to see more clearly. Get packed – we're leaving.'

As the words rolled from his tongue so his eyes cleared, his vision returning.

'I've been so blind Roz but I can see clearly now for the first time. It's going to be okay. We're going to Lionsgate. The Great One is expecting us.'

She squealed in delight and threw her arms around him, kissing his cheek.

They knew they were risking their lives. This could be a trap but it was a risk they were willing to take. They had to trust the Great One to rescue them. No one else could.

⌘

Aislinn was tired and hungry. Her dreams left her disturbed, her mind reeling. She felt weak and cold and she hugged her knees to her chest.

'I can't do this anymore. I'm so tired and the silence in this place is killing me. I feel as though I'm going mad. Great One, Ziah – please help me. I know you can,' she pleaded.

She felt her cold body warm up as though someone had wrapped her in giant arms. She even glanced around to see if Ryder had entered the cell – so thick was the presence. Then it came to her. The man in her dream was Ziah. Of course! He was the Key Keeper - she remembered how important the recovery of those keys was to him and she would recognize them anywhere. The keys for the door in her dream were Ziah's keys – the very keys she helped him rescue. She giggled in sheer relief. He needed to bring them to her. Papa had told her that the Great One could always hear the cries of his followers. He never let them down. More than ever she hoped this were true. The Great One had helped her many times over the last couple of weeks and deep in her heart she believed that he would hear her and pass her message on to Ziah.

'Great One,' she began tentatively, her whispers echoing around the stony walls, 'I'm sorry I just disappeared to get Mitchell without consulting you first. It was a stupid mistake to make and now I am paying for it. I do believe though that you can hear me and that you love me enough to help me. I need Ziah to bring me the keys. I know somehow that they are my way out of here. I wouldn't be surprised if it was you speaking to me in my dream last night. Thank you – you're the best,' she finished feeling peaceful and hopeful.

## CHAPTER 27

# REDEMPTION

*No one is ever beyond redemption, if they choose to walk that path*
— Mitch Rowland, Eternity's Reach

'SHE did it Father,' he yelled triumphantly. 'She's called for the keys!'

He grabbed hold of his father's arms, dancing in a circle with childlike delight.

The old man and his son beamed at each other.

'Of course she did, Ziah,' he laughed. 'Get Nuada, Regent, Serena and Ryder ready. I'll find Aedan – he won't want to miss this adventure,' he chuckled.

Ziah rushed off to find the team who would be a part of Aislinn's freedom. They had all been looking over her in some way or another and this would be the final triumph. Things were beginning to look up on all fronts. He skipped off like a little boy who had some exciting news to share and his father watched him lovingly as he went. That boy was a joy and had accomplished more in his life than many realized. News spread quickly of Aislinn's call for the keys. The air was electric with excitement and Mac and Imogene quickly headed to the Great One's court. They too had heard the news, but they felt a little more anxious as they did not yet realize the significance of the keys.

'At last the moment we have all been waiting for,' they heard Aedan saying as they entered the court. 'Finally that miserable old creature will be taken down and we will have the opportunity to relax for a bit. I feel we deserve a sabbatical after all his plots and ploys,'

Everyone chuckled at Aedan's sense of humour. They would all be glad when this was over.

A knock at the door changed their focus briefly as a tall warrior dressed in a purple robe entered the court.

'There's a man and a woman at the gate,' he said quickly. 'They have a little boy with them. They claim its Mitchell Hamilton.'

Imogene felt weak at the knees and she gasped aloud. She dared not hope too much – they had been so disappointed over the last few weeks and each time she thought there was nothing left of her heart to break, another little piece would be torn off again.

'Well what are you waiting for,' the Great One replied. 'Bring them in – I've been expecting them.'

Morelock and Rozanne entered the court with a mixture of trepidation and awe. They had never seen a more beautiful place and they gazed in wonder at all they saw. As they approached the Great One their eyes became downcast and all they had done for the Dark Lord seemed magnified in this place. Would they be punished for Ziah's death? Was this a trick to get them here? They could not bring themselves to look at the people who would surely accuse them. Rozanne held out her arms, barely able to hold a squirming Mitchell, waiting for someone to take him. Imogene rushed forward and clasped the little boy as though she would never let him go. His sweet scent pervaded her nostrils and she breathed deeply taking in the smell she had missed so severely.

'Mama,' the little boy said as though she hadn't been gone for more than a day, and he nuzzled his head into her neck.

It was too much for Imogene – she sobbed in relief and pent up emotion. Rozanne watched, feeling worse than before, but also glad they had made the decision to come. No matter what happened now, it was worth it to see mother and son reunited. How she wished she could experience love like that.

⌘

Legion waited for word on Morelock. Falstaff had informed him that he had not been into his chamber that morning. This was uncharacteristic behaviour for Morelock and it made him uneasy. Morelock was extremely dedicated to his work and took great pride in all he did. He had high hopes for the young wizard – many new spells would come from his chamber that would benefit the Dark Lord. Where was he?

A knock at the door dragged him from his reverie.

'Enter,' he growled.

'There is no further news Master,' Falstaff stated flatly. 'It's as if they have vanished into thin air. Someone has been out to their cottage but there is no sign of them.'

'Send out some scouts and keep looking. I want to know when they are found,' he said tersely.

⌘

Down in the dungeon Aislinn sang softly to herself. Since calling out to the Great One and Ziah, she felt completely different. She felt calm and curiously courageous. It seemed ridiculous in the circumstances, but she even felt joyful. It was as though she knew deep down that everything was going to be all right. That sickly fear she felt for the Dark Lord had even disappeared. Now she only felt angry, determined never to be intimidated by him again. She had allowed herself to feel weak and manipulated but that was the past and this was now. She would never surrender to him and she vowed to show no fear no matter what he did to her. As she sang her spirits lifted and her courage multiplied.

⌘

Rozanne and Imogene sat together in the dining hall drinking a hot, sweet drink they called 'nectar tea' in Lionsgate. Rozanne felt ashamed and waited for Imogene to vent her anger at having her child given away like a disposable commodity.

'Firstly,' Imogene said slowly, 'I want to thank you for taking such good care of Mitchell.'

Rozanne looked surprised– she was caught completely off guard.

'I suppose,' Imogene continued 'that if he had to be anywhere I can be grateful it was not in the Dark Lord's castle. Secondly, thank you for bringing him back to us. I can imagine it was one of the hardest decisions for you to make.'

Rozanne had no words. Large tears traced their way down her cheeks at the gracious response of this woman.

She expected anger and loathing and instead she was receiving love and forgiveness.

'Why aren't you angry with us?'

'I have no right to judge you Rozanne. All of us have facets of our personality that aren't perfect. I too have had to journey to this place to learn that our mistakes do not have to define us. They can be the very things that propel us forward to greater heights in the future. The Great One loves us despite our mistakes and so I will always endeavour to love others the same way. That is what I have learned here in Lionsgate. Love is a most powerful thing. It conquers every other emotion and most of all, it never fails. We each have our own challenges in life –it's how we respond to them and the choices we make that count; but once you have experienced this kind of love, you can never be the same again.'

Rozanne looked at Imogene with gratitude and admiration.

'I hope I learn to love this way too.'

⌘

'News has come at last Master,' Falstaff said, a hint of glee in his voice. Finally his competition was gone and he felt delighted that Morelock would never fill his shoes.

'Morelock and Rozanne have left Griswold. They were seen by some families crossing the border.'

'Where were they going?' Legion asked, dread curling itself around his spine in a vice-like grip.

The reply stabbed Legion's heart with final, humiliating betrayal.

'Lionsgate.'

⌘

Aislinn realized as she wrung her hands that she was wearing the truth ring. She had forgotten that she had placed it on her hand so as not to lose it. The glasses had been left in the little cottage in her room, but the ring had come with her. It gave her some comfort to know that a part of the Great One was with her. Her musings were interrupted by the lock of the door being opened. As the door creaked on its hinges, she waited in anticipation for the one who would come through that door. She had prepared herself for this moment mentally, but the reality of it was quite something else.

He stood there, a menacing black vulture. His eyes cold and furious stared at her expecting to see her cringe and cower before him. She did not.

'So dear Aislinn, you have abused my hospitality and now you find yourself here in this place. You will never get out of here alive, my dear.'

Aislinn twisted the ring noticing it change from its neutral colour to a deep yellow. It gave her hope. The Dark Lord's words were not true. She ignored his jibe.

'Is Mitchell okay?'

Legion looked surprised at her gall and sneered. 'You won't ever see him again. He's been sent to wizardry school. The younger they take them the easier it is for them to learn the dark side.'

Again the ring turned a deep yellow and Aislinn sighed in relief.

'You won't get away with this,' she challenged. 'I have called Ziah and he is coming for me.'

Legion laughed but his eyes held a measure of surprise and fear.

'There's nothing Ziah can do for you but I have a proposition for you. You may redeem yourself by becoming my wife and working alongside me to make Griswold the most powerful kingdom, or you can choose to die as a traitor. I will not be mocked among my own people and you have made a fool of me Aislinn. Nonetheless I will give you an opportunity to redeem yourself.'

She looked surprised at his offer. She had expected death as her only choice.

'I'll give you time to think,' he said, walking out the door.

Aislinn slumped down on the hard floor. It was cold, but she felt good. She had stood her ground without fear and she had learned that Mitchell was safe and that she was not going to die here from the truth ring. She closed her eyes and thanked the Great One for being with her.

⌘

Legion paced up and down his chamber. He had expected her to cower in fear from him and yet she had shown courage. He did not understand why she had so much confidence. Surely she didn't believe that Ziah was really coming for her? That was absurd.

It infuriated him that he still wanted her so badly and more so that she would not be coerced into marrying him with the threat of death. It irked him that she was a thorn in his flesh – a weakness he could not control. He had to have her and the more she resisted the greater his desire to tame her became.

Legion was used to getting his own way. He wanted her and he would have her – no matter what.

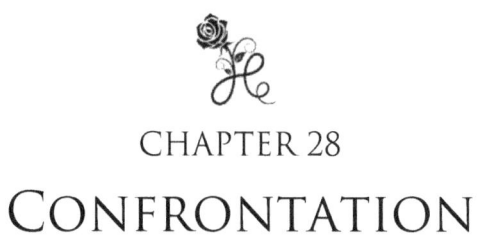

## CHAPTER 28
# CONFRONTATION

*The harder the conflict, the more glorious the triumph*
— Thomas Paine

THE RATTLING dungeon door and shaking walls woke Aislinn from deep sleep. What was happening? It felt as though the earth were moving. Was it an earth rumble as they were commonly known? It would be ironic if she were to die in a rumble, crushed by these stony dungeon walls. The dungeon door popped open like a cork from a bottle with a whooshing sound and Aislinn expected guards to come running in to prevent her escape. The door remained eerily empty. As she stood staring at the open door unable to believe her good fortune, a silhouette appeared in the doorway.

'Come on Aislinn, you called for the keys and I've come.'

'Ziah!' She rushed to him and wrapped her arms around him. 'I knew you would come.'

'Can we leave the reunion till later?' another voice chipped in. 'Somehow I don't think our arrival will go unnoticed.'

There stood Aedan, beaming at Aislinn with Nuada, Regent, Ryder and Serena all close behind. They all looked delighted to see her unharmed and in good spirits.

'Oh my goodness, what have you done to the guards?' she asked giggling. They were frozen like statues, unable to move. The one guard was scratching his rear end and they all chuckled at how ridiculous he looked.

'They are a little stuck for now,' Aedan added giggling with her, 'but they will be okay in about an hour or two.'

'Come,' said Ziah 'let's make our way back to Lionsgate.'

As they turned to move up the dungeon stairs, they felt, rather than perceived the presence of evil that flowed into the icy corridor where they were standing. Their presence had not gone unnoticed in the Dark Lord's castle.

'So you dared to come back here did you?' They all knew that voice. He sounded confident, yet his eyes held uncertainty and his fear was not lost on Ziah or his companions.

Aislinn felt no fear now, as she had endured much over the past weeks and she felt safer with them than she had in a long while.

'So we meet again.' Ziah smiled at his discomfort. 'I've come to get back something that does not belong to you,' he stated indicating Aislinn. She looked at the Dark Lord, pity in her eyes mixed with anger for the evil he had done. It was not the anger that bothered Legion as he fed off it, but the pity felt like a knife wound. He could not tolerate being pitied by anyone – pity was for weak people who had nothing. He did not want to be perceived that way by anyone.

'You're a sad person,' Aislinn blurted out. 'Why do you allow your heart to be like stone? All of us have experienced pain in life, yet not all of us choose to be crippled by it. But you - you not only became crippled, you try to cripple as many others as you can and that is just pathetic.'

Legion could barely contain his fury at the girl's words. He pulled Ziah aside whispering maliciously.

'Coming back here is rather a brave move, don't you think?'

'There's nothing more you can do to me. I've beaten death. After all, you agreed to trade her and her siblings for me and I overcame the hardest obstacle you put before me. I did as you asked– you have no right over them now.'

'Yes you did. Sacrifice is part of your weakness. It will be your undoing now.'

'It wasn't about sacrifice. It was about love,' Ziah countered.

Legion scoffed. 'Love – is for the weak.'

'Love is more powerful than fear will ever be,' Ziah challenged.

'If that is the case then prove it. Give me permission Ziah to put your team to the test, to show everyone in Griswold that what you believe is a lie.'

'We don't have to pass a test to leave. I don't really see how you can stop us Sephtis,' Ziah countered.

'I may not be able to stop you but we will certainly try. Do you want to take the chance of some of your people getting hurt or killed? I give you my word that if they overcome the challenges, I will let you go.'

Ziah was confident his team could fight them off but keeping Aislinn safe was his first priority. He needed to buy them some time. He also wanted the people of Griswold to see that love never failed – that goodness triumphed over evil and what better opportunity to do it than showing up the Dark Lord in front of those he deceived.

'I will allow this test – I'm confident we can overcome the obstacles you throw our way. Be warned though, if you go back on your word you will reap destruction in Griswold and that will be your undoing.'

Legion turned back to the others who were curiously watching the heated exchange between the two rivals.

'We'll take this up to the courtyard,' he announced to them with confidence, 'where your team will compete in a series of challenges. If you are able to conquer the challenges set before you by my witches and wizards, before the hour glass empties out, then you may leave with Aislinn Hamilton and I will never bother the Hamilton family again.'

'So be it,' said Ziah with steely determination. Maybe this would finally teach this arrogant creature a lesson and humiliate him in front of the whole of Griswold. After today everyone would see him for who he really was.

'Why are we doing this Ziah?' Aedan asked incredulous. 'We could fight our way out of here right now. He is toying with us, making us look like fools.'

'That is true my friend,' he responded. 'Just trust me with this. If we leave now his wizards and goblins will try to stop us and we will have a battle to wage before we get Aislinn out of here. If we defeat him at his own game then his people will see him for who he really is. I want love to win this war, not bloodshed.'

Aedan nodded.

News of Ziah's magical escape from death travelled fast in the Dark Lord's ranks. Entering the courtyard they found it teeming with evil goblins and creatures of every kind, curious to see the two teams pitted against one another. The air was electric with anticipation and excitement. Never had the people of Griswold seen the Dark Lord in direct battle with the Great One's forces. This would be talked about for generations. Goblins wagered with one another as to the outcome.

'The rules are such,' declared Legion. 'Three of you will complete a challenge I select and every challenge has to be mastered to win Aislinn's freedom.'

'That's fine with us,' Ziah responded.

'I choose the golden haired woman to complete challenge number one,' the Dark Lord announced looking at Serena.

'You will attempt to solve this riddle.'

Ziah smiled. It should be a fairly simple challenge for Serena. She was known for her great wisdom in Lionsgate.

The riddle was read from an old, weathered parchment that had seen better days.

*An eye that can never see*

*The beauty of the world to be*

*Pass through it to the other side*

*And find the crystal it will hide*

*Treasure that is hard to see*

*Unless you look so carefully*

*Behind the curtain it is concealed*

*Its beauty and light will secrets reveal.*

Serena read the riddle again and drew aside. The rules of the competition forbade her to get any help from her team. She had to figure this out herself.

'Your time begins now,' said Legion turning over the enormous hour glass.

'You have an hour to complete it.'

'Great One,' she whispered, 'you're not part of this team so I'm not breaking any rules - you are the giver of all wisdom. I need you to show me what this means and to direct me to the right place.'

She spoke softly to him, her mind clearing and a picture forming in her imagination. It was of a clearing in a forest she had passed through in Griswold.

'I'll be back before the hour glass runs out.' She disappeared as fast as she could through the castle gates. The amazing thing about being one of the Great One's team was that travel was instant when you wished it so.

In the twinkling of an eye, she was standing in the clearing she had seen in her vision. Grimwood Forest was usually a dangerous, dark place. Today however, the sun streamed through the trees and danced with dappled light on the soft, mossy ground.

An eye that cannot see would be a blind eye and certainly would not see the beauty around it, but then a real eye is not able to be passed through. This must refer to another kind of eye, she mused, trying to work out the first part of the riddle. What other eyes are there?

She closed her eyes again and allowed the Great One to fill her mind with images. She knew the answer - it was the eye of a needle. But how would she pass through it and where was it? She thought hard of all the places in Griswold that could be relevant. The only logical conclusion was a place called Needlepoint. It was near the top of a steep mountain pass – a cave that had the opening like a needle's eye, but it was extremely difficult to get there. Very few knew how to find the path that led to the cave as it was situated in an enchanted forest. There was a legend that great riches could be found in the cave at Needlepoint. The Dark Lord's wizards had ensured that many a greedy traveller looking for the treasure had never found their way out of the forest ever again. Serena knew she could get there instantly if she only knew the way, but unfortunately she had no idea how to proceed.

'What now Great One?' she asked frustrated.

The soft nuzzling and noise of a creature in the clearing caught Serena by surprise. Looking up she saw a unicorn shaking its mane. It appeared to be beckoning her. Serena laughed and thanked the Great One. These beautiful creatures were few and far between in Griswold now as they had hidden in the forests when evil made its home here. They knew every part of the forests. Serena straddled the strong unicorn and held onto its silken mane.

'Can you take me to Needlepoint?'

The unicorn turned, galloping off into the forest, Serena clinging to its flowing mane. The climb was steep and she clung to the unicorn tightly, her hair pulled and clawed by the branches of the trees, as though they were trying to pull her from her mount and swallow her up. At last they alighted at the top of the pass where the needle-like eye rose out of the ground into the sky as a rocky outcrop. She dismounted, patting the unicorn affectionately.

'Thanks girl,' she whispered, 'I can find my way back.'

Entering the cave Serena became aware of screaming, shrieking voices within the dark recesses. They were frightening and eerie. She covered her ears, moving through the cave as quickly as she could. She averted her eyes from the numerous skeletal remains that piled up along the cave walls – she guessed that some fortune hunters had found their way after all, only to come to a grisly end.

'Who dares enter my cave?'

A gruff, angry creature stepped out blocking Serena's way. He was at least seven foot tall, his face and body covered in wiry hair. He looked like a wolf man and his hands had sharp claws where his nails should be. Serena guessed this was how many men had met their end whilst searching for the treasure at Needlepoint. She shuddered at the thought.

'I'm Serena – the Dark Lord has set me a challenge to find something in this cave.'

'He obviously doesn't like you very much then. Have you not seen what happens to those who dare to steal from me?' He glanced at the pile of bones on the dusty cave floor.

'Yes, I've seen the bones but that can't scare me off – this challenge is a matter of life and death for someone very important to me. If I don't help her the Dark Lord will kill her.'

'You would trade your own life to save someone else? That's rather noble of you Serena.'

'Please Mr....'

'The name's Tremblood, but you can call me Trem. I tell you what Serena – I like you far more than any of the greedy self-seeking men who have come here before. You're the first with someone else's welfare at heart – that is rare indeed. I'm not usually a sentimental creature but I am not a complete brute either. I will let you pass safely if you can give me something of value in return for the treasure you seek. It's only fair to pay for what you take.'

'Of course Trem. What did you have in mind?'

That beautiful jewel entwined in your hair will make a nice payment.'

Serena smiled – there were many more jewels where this came from. She reached up and pulled the clasp from her shiny mane.

'There we go Trem – it's all yours.' She left him admiring the shining jewel, turning it over in his clawed hands.

She emerged from the cave into a grotto full of giant, lush plants and a cascading waterfall. The grotto was not dark, neither was it light. She looked around but could see nothing that looked valuable or treasure-like. What had the riddle said? It urged her to find treasure that was concealed, referring to a curtain. Serena looked around, drawing aside a mossy curtain that draped itself over the rock face. Nothing! What else could it be? She stood, pondering the riddle when a shaft of light poured through the needle eye, lighting up the small waterfall before her like a sparkling diamond. The light danced on the water, revealing another small cave behind it. This must be it. The water was the curtain referred to in the riddle - she was sure of it. She scrambled behind the falls, trying not to slip on the mossy stones. The rocks were damp and slick before her. The sun's rays penetrated the waterfall, sending rays of luminous light dancing in various directions. She marvelled at the beauty admiring the reflections. This rock glinted and reflected and sparkled like a jewel - it was different to the rock outside the cave. Then Serena saw what she was looking for. She stretched out her hand, pulling hard at the shiny stone as it loosened in her grasp. She gazed in wonder at the shining crystal that came loose in her hand. She would not have seen it if the sun had not shone through the cave, but she guessed the Great One knew that. He certainly could organize things perfectly. People in this world called it coincidence, but she knew better. Carefully she placed the crystal rock into her saddle pouch and made her way back through the cave, thanking Trem as she left.

She had less than a quarter hour to get back to the Dark Lord's castle before her time ran out and she was most grateful not to be Tremblood's next meal.

Aislinn felt nervous as she watched the sand running through the hour glass, a silent threat that mocked as each grain fell. If Serena failed this task, they would all suffer. None of the others seemed concerned and Ziah smiled at her reassuringly. The Dark Lord looked more and more confident that this challenge may be over before it began. He was counting on Tremblood devouring the helpless woman should she find the path to Needlepoint. His goblins and creatures were restless in anticipation.

As the last few grains of sand trickled through the hourglass Serena appeared, making her way over to Legion. She stood before him, removing the crystal from her pouch.

'I believe this is the treasure you speak of,' she said handing Legion the crystal. 'Oh, and Trem sends his regards,' she added cheekily.

His face clouded, annoyed at her success.

'I see you have conquered the task, but there are still two challenges to come. We shall see. The second challenge is a challenge of power. I choose the flame-haired man to compete.'

Aedan smiled. At last it was his moment to silence this evil once and for all.

'My wizard will cast a spell, and you need to produce something that will neutralize that which he has created,' said Legion.

Aedan had a twinkle in his eye. This challenge was perfect for him.

Falstaff stepped forward chanting a spell. This was his moment to make the Master proud. A venomous snake materialized and slithered toward Aedan, rearing up, ready to strike its target.

'Nasty,' Aedan murmured unperturbed as the onlookers all backed away in fear.

He struck the ground with the heel of his foot, the snake transforming into a lizard that scuttled off as fast as its four legs could carry it. Falstaff looked momentarily impressed then a little annoyed at how easily Aedan had dismissed his magic. There was not even an ounce of fear in the man. Immediately he chanted another spell that covered Aedan in boils and sores that oozed a sickening green substance. Maybe now he would feel a little more fearful.

'This is becoming a little personal,' he complained to Falstaff. 'I don't take too kindly to that.'

The onlookers watched, startled as his skin began to glow, appearing like fire, becoming so bright that everyone shielded their eyes from the glaring light of his body. When it seemed everyone would be struck with blindness his body returned to normal, but it was no longer covered in sores. It was charged with power that had the little goblins gasping in admiration and fear.

'How did he do that,' they all chorused.

'Silence!' roared the Dark Lord.

Falstaff was visibly disconcerted now. He prided himself on his wizardry talents and this man was making him look like an amateur. It was time for the trump card. Chanting aloud he invoked his final test. A loud rumbling filled the skies, a combination of a rushing and explosive sound. Everyone gazed up into the clouds, curious but dreading what would soon descend upon them. A ball of fire shot down from the heavens, scorching a wagon in the courtyard and sending goblins and people running with shrieks of terror. Fascination turned to fear as Draco swooped over the castle wall and into the courtyard, his fearsome, powerful limbs shaking the foundations of the stonework. Ziah grabbed Aislinn, shielding her as she trembled fearfully. Draco had eyes only for Aedan as his fiery red hair glinted in the sunlight. Everyone had hidden in places that would provide little protection, if any at all, but Aedan stood his ground facing the menacing dragon.

'Come to papa,' he called taunting. Nothing seemed to scare the man!

The dragon lunged forward clumsily, trying to manoeuvre his huge body in the confined courtyard, as Aedan transformed himself into a whirlwind. He spun around the dragon at such a speed, causing him to run in circles as though he were a dog chasing his tail. When he was sure the dragon was disoriented, he looked up to the sky and shouted.

The heavens responded, opening like a stage curtain for the final scene, a bolt of lightning snaking down from the wispy summer clouds striking the confused dragon between its eyes. Draco's huge body shuddered and slumped to the floor shaking the walls as it did so. There was a deathly hush - the goblins realizing the Dark Lord had been defeated yet again. This man was far more powerful than their wizard– he had power that clearly came from another source. Even the heavens obeyed him. Falstaff flushed crimson, dreading the recourse that would surely come from the Master.

Legion realized that trying to outwit the Great One's team was futile – he should have known better. He may have been overly confident, but the final card he would play would surely cause the team to fail.

# CHAPTER 29
# TRUTH

*I believe that unarmed truth and unconditional love will have the final word in reality. This is why right, temporarily defeated, is stronger than evil triumphant*

— Martin Luther King, Jr.

'THE next challenge is a truth challenge and I select Aislinn to compete.'

'I object,' Ziah interjected. 'You said our team would compete for Aislinn, so surely she can't be considered to compete for her own freedom.'

'As far as I can tell she has not indicated to me that she is part of my team, which clearly makes her part of your team and therefore she is eligible to compete in the challenges. Are you afraid she will fail Ziah? I thought love could never fail?'

Ziah looked angry momentarily. This man was a scheming liar through and through – this was nonsense.

'It's okay Ziah,' Aislinn said stepping forward. 'I think I can handle this challenge.'

Ziah was a little concerned, but seeing her confidence he smiled at her.

'All right Aislinn, if you feel you can do it then we believe in you.'

The others nodded in agreement, calling out words of encouragement.

Legion handed Aislinn the crystal that Serena had returned from the cave.

'Look into the crystal and you'll see pictures before you. Each scenario will require you to judge whether it is the truth or a lie. There will be three pictures. If you get even one wrong, then you fail the challenge.'

Aislinn gazed into the crystal looking carefully to see what it would reveal. It became murky then cleared revealing their little house in Griswold and the attackers closing in silently on the family. Aislinn gasped, recognizing the awful event that started this whole drama for their family. Could she bear to watch this again? She willed herself as the men silently lit their home. She watched the cloaked man draw his sword and slash her father viciously. His face filled the crystal and for the first time she saw his true identity - it was the face of her father's friend, Cillian. No it couldn't be, everything in her mind screamed. They were like family. Legion smirked seeing her pale, shocked face. He knew the Great One well enough to know that he would protect the Hamilton Children from this truth. Seeing her hurt expression gave him incredible satisfaction. He would hurt her as much as he could.

Aislinn was tempted to cry out that it was a lie but she remembered the ring on her finger and looked down at it tentatively. She could not allow her emotion or pain to rush her answers – she must trust the ring. She hoped with all her heart the stone would be gleaming yellow, but as she looked she saw that it was a deep shimmering purple. The pain of that ripped at her soul.

'Well,' said Legion menacingly, 'what is it - the truth or a lie?'

Aislinn's voice trembled and the pain on her face was evident as she stammered, 'it's a…a… a …the truth.'

Legion flushed angrily but nodded his head. Aedan's fury at his cruelty made his hair and eyes glow. The Great One had kept this truth from the Hamilton children for a reason and now this evil creature had tormented her again. Oh, how he wished he could crush him.

'The next scene will appear shortly so pay attention.'

Aislinn peered into the murky crystal again. She saw Mitchell playing outside Rozanne and Morelock's home. In childish curiosity he wandered off chasing a butterfly, oblivious to where he was going. He followed the flitting creature into the trees at the bottom of the field. As he ran alongside the little stream, reaching out trying to catch the elusive butterfly, he tripped over a protruding root and tumbled headlong into the icy water. His little body struggled but he was unable to swim and soon he lay still and cold, his face down in the water. Aislinn gasped, all colour draining from her beautiful face.

*No, it can't be true. Please don't let it be true*, she prayed silently to herself. She felt shock take hold of her body – fear coursing through her veins like a deadly drug.

She was too afraid to look at the ring but knew she had to. She glanced down, terrified of what she might see. Still, she had brought them all to this place and to this challenge and she must not allow her courage to desert her now, no matter what she saw. She wept out loud, relief flooding her when she saw the yellow stone gleaming.

'It's a lie,' she spat out with loathing at the Dark Lord. 'Mitchell's not dead. I would know it if he was.'

'Not bad Aislinn,' said Legion looking impressed at her ability. He'd been convinced she would crumble under the emotional strain and he couldn't help but admire her feistiness and spirit. He was playing mind games with her, but she held her resolve. Had he known that it was the ring giving her the answers he would have been less impressed. The truth was that without the ring, she would have been undone.

'The final challenge will surely test you. It's not over yet,' he spat menacingly.

Aislinn just wanted it to be over. She looked again into the crystal. What she saw confused her momentarily. It was not of the past or present – in fact it wasn't anything she recognized. She saw a young woman in childbirth. The woman was in agony as she laboured to bring her baby to birth. She cried out in pain and held fast the hand of a young man beside her. She could not see their faces but he mopped her brow, worried at his inability to help his young wife. It was clear that he adored her.

'Come on Aislinn, you can do it,' he encouraged her.

She realized in surprise that this was the future she was seeing. She watched, fascinated at the event wondering about her future and the young man that was part of the vision she saw. This soon turned to horror as she watched herself haemorrhage and bleed out on the bed. The baby was stillborn and her husband sobbed as he hugged her lifeless body. This was horrific. *Surely she wouldn't die that young and her baby ... not her baby too?*

She looked at Legion, shock etched on her face.

'Truth or a lie?' His mocking eyes challenged her. He could see her uncertainty – her fear and distress at what she had seen.

'How can I possibly know the answer to the future?' she snapped.

'So you surrender then?' He mocked.

'Not a chance of that happening,' she retorted. Even if she got this answer wrong she would go down fighting.

She looked at the ring, emotionally depleted - she would not give him the satisfaction of seeing her crumble. Surely the ring would help her. To her dismay it showed no colour at all. It was clear and Aislinn looked at Ziah, panic in her eyes. She didn't know the answer. Not even the ring knew the answer – they were sunk.

'It's all right Aislinn, he encouraged seeing uncertainty written all over her face. 'Go with your heart. What is it telling you?' he said.

'I don't know,' she cried. 'How can anyone know the future?'

'Remember what I've always told you when times have been tough,' Regent said.

She thought hard. She and Regent had shared many conversations over the last few weeks. Which conversation was he talking about and what had he repeated to her more than once? Now was not the time to play riddle games with her. Her mind was in overdrive.

Whenever she was afraid or unsure Regent always said to her, *'Nothing's impossible for those who believe.'* That must be it.

'I think,' she said slowly, terrified she may have the wrong answer, 'that it's a lie. I trust the Great One, and I believe he will keep me safe and that nothing will be impossible for me as long as I believe.'

Legion flushed. He was furious. He hadn't reduced her to an insecure wreck. She still believed in the Great One and had chosen him above anything else despite all she had gone through. He had failed again. She had secured her freedom with her belief. There was no more he could do to her – she had made herself one with them and he could not touch her any longer. His hatred grew deeper – he had lost the one thing he truly wanted besides the Great One's power.

Ziah hugged her fiercely, delighted at her insight and being brave enough to follow her heart.

'Remember,' he whispered, 'no one can plan your future. What you believe and declare will bring it into being.'

'Get out of my castle.'

Legion could not bear to look at them one moment longer, his fury barely disguised

He had been defeated by the faith of a young girl – it was a bitter blow and a huge humiliation.

'We'll leave, but if you ever try and attack the Hamilton family again, we will be back and we won't be so tolerant the next time.'

'By the way Legion,' Aislinn added, 'Cillian did not kill my parents – you couldn't even get that right. The Great One saved them because he is one who loves greatly. You are not half the man he is.'

Legion turned, marching out of the courtyard, back to his chambers where he would replay the events over and over in his head. He needed a strong glass of wine to quench the growing feeling of humiliation and defeat that his subjects had witnessed. He would have strategize a new plan of action. He would never give up – his hatred ran too deep, even though deep down he knew that he could never win.

CHAPTER 30

# TRIUMPH

*I learned that courage was not the absence of fear, but the triumph over it. The brave man is not he who does not feel afraid, but he who conquers that fear*

— Nelson Mandela

THE group approached Lionsgate, chatting animatedly about all they had experienced over the last few weeks. It had been an adventure and Aislinn was pleased it was coming to an end. She felt exhausted, exhilarated and grateful for the companions she travelled with. Ziah shared the news that Mitchell was safely back with their family in Lionsgate and the weight of guilt she felt eased.

'Why couldn't the truth ring give me an answer for the future?' she asked Ziah when she had a moment alone with him as they wandered behind everyone along the footpath.

'The ring can tell us only what is present or past truth, but it doesn't predict the future because each person creates their own destiny through their thoughts and beliefs. The Dark Lord wanted you to believe the worst and to live in fear for your future. That's what he does – he tries to bring fear to man so that their future is one of hopelessness and pain.'

'Does that mean I control my destiny?'

'Yes it does, with the choices you make, so dream big Aislinn,' he said smiling. 'Many people believe that their future and destiny is a very narrow path – a bit like this path we are on,' he said pointing at the stones.

'In fact even your parents believed that until recently,' he chuckled.

'What is our future like then?' she asked keen to know the answer.

'It's so much bigger than that Aislinn. It's like living in a beautiful garden with amazing trees and plants and places to explore but then being told that you may not step off the path to experience the soft grass under your feet or to smell and pick flowers. Some people are so busy following the rules that they never leave the path and they miss out on so many amazing experiences. Don't let anyone tell you where you can play in the garden of life Aislinn. You make your choices and decide who you are. You are meant to be an individual. How else can you make a difference and love those around you unless you are free to be yourself.'

'I've also been wondering why we had to complete those challenges to defeat the Dark Lord. Aedan alone could have taken them all out.'

He smiled at her. She already knew the answer as she had lived it out.

'Yes, we could have beaten him in battle, but sometimes fighting is not the answer. When you discovered who you are, you won the greatest battle of all. You made it impossible for the Dark Lord to hold you in fear and this brings great freedom. No man should ever have control over another. We are all valuable Aislinn.

'Thank you Ziah – for being there for me. I love you.'

'And I you,' he said suddenly smiling and swinging her around in a circle.

They fell onto the soft grass laughing as they watched the clouds.

'Knowing you is fun,' she sighed content.

'Just enjoy the whole garden Aislinn.'

The reception that greeted them as they entered the great hall was jubilant. Trumpets sounded and cheers of joy greeted them from every corner of the hall. Mac and Imogene rushed to their daughter, embracing her as though they would never let her go. They had been so worried for her and now they realized how much she had matured and grown in the last few weeks. She had been a young girl a few weeks ago and now she was a young woman – she had made them proud.

The Great One watched them joyfully, pleasure in his heart. He considered them all his family – each and every one of them. The greatest joy to him though, was that the Hamilton family had discovered treasures that went beyond riches. They had been on a quest – not of their own choosing, but they had found what they were looking for. Each of them had experienced an awakening. They had found their real selves – each family member in a different way, but each richer for who they had become. They had discovered relationship with one another in greater measure but even more so with the Great One himself. They had also discovered freedom to be themselves and to live in it. They had found the ability to dream bigger than they ever imagined or expected. Yes, there would be many adventures to come and many challenges too, but they had found truth and strength to move forward from the past. They had found true friends in Lionsgate.

# EPILOGUE

'WHERE do you want me to put this thatch Mac?' Eion asked as he staggered forward, his arms laden with the golden stalks.

'Just there will do fine.' Mac smiled at the enthusiastic young man.

It had taken them a while to rebuild a life and home for themselves, but with the help of their new friends it had been made a lot easier. Now, they lived in a quiet place called Sherbrooke. Mac had gone back to thatching once they had left Griswold and he felt satisfied and content with their life. Eion was a worthy apprentice who worked hard, and each day the two men began work before the sun was up so that they had time to talk and build their friendship over the evening meal the families always ate together.

They were very fond of this young couple who had courageously followed their hearts and consciences. Eion, previously known as Morelock, had decided he wanted a new name. He no longer wanted to be known by his old name - that man was 'dead' – someone who was a pawn in the Dark Lord's evil chess game. He and Rozanne had settled on the name Eion, after his great-grandfather. It was especially relevant as it meant The Great One is gracious – something they had seen firsthand from the day they had arrived in Lionsgate and they still saw it every day of their lives. It was a new name for a new life and a fresh start. He had once been a man who had used his power for darkness and evil – helping to build the Dark Lord's kingdom – that is until he met the Great One. They had decided to make their new home in the same village as Mac and Imogene so that they could learn as much as they could from them about the Great One. This was all so new to them and they were hungry for truth which Mac and Imogene couldn't satisfy fast enough. They had found more than friendship with the Hamilton's – they had acceptance for who they were.

Rozanne was swollen with the baby that she carried and everyone was excited about the precious gift that would soon come. They had been amazed when she had fallen pregnant after years of barrenness, but Imogene had put it down to the fact that Lionsgate was a place of life and love – a place where dreams are made. They learned again of the Great One's goodness in granting them the dream they had yearned for. That's what they loved so much about him – he never held their past against them – he only ever encouraged them to a greater hope and future.

'Mac,' a voice called from behind. It was a welcome interruption from binding straw.

'Aedan,' he exclaimed spinning around at his friend's voice. 'It's so good to see you again?'

'Good to see you too my friend,'

He hugged Mac fiercely to his broad chest.

'You look well! Are you ready to come with us on a new adventure? We need your help – there's a family that have lost everything in a fire and we thought we could give them a hand to rebuild their home.'

'Well I can relate to that,' Mac laughed. 'I'll be with you in a moment. I just need to let Imogene know. I'll see if we have any leftover bread and some blankets to spare too.'

'Send her our love,' Aedan shouted after him as he raced into the house, eager anticipation written all over his face.

He was living the dream now. He loved helping the Great One, working side by side with Aedan and his friends. This was what he had been created for. Never again would he lead a community with laws and rules for living – instead he was determined to live life with people as friends and to laugh with them in joyous times and cry with them when they needed it. The Great One had taught them the meaning of true love, true faith and true hope. That was the way it was always meant to be. Helping people in a practical way was far more beneficial than teaching laws and lessons for life. Actions really did speak louder than words and Mac and his family were determined that this was how they would live their life now.

*It's strange*, Mac thought, *how the prophecy had turned out to be true after all.* Initially they understood it to mean they would teach people how to live when what they really needed to do was just live and let people learn by their example.

He chuckled as he entered the house at how things had worked out after all.

Imogene watched from the doorway of the thatched cottage as the men made their way over the hill – off on another adventure. Each day was different and each adventure taught them something new. There was no expectation other than the sense of satisfaction they got from every person they cared for and helped. She felt grateful as she watched her husband and best friend walking with the red-haired Aedan and dark Regent. He was a different man now – no longer needing to prove his success. He had found security in knowing who he was and walking in it each day at a time. The sun rose up over the hill in a ball of glory and warmth. The past was gone and could never be changed, but she would not have wished to alter one detail of their journey and the love they had gained. It was another new day dawning for them all - each day a new awakening of living a life of truth and love.

⌘

The Great One looked in His mirror and smiled knowingly. They were following their dreams – it had been a painful process for them but they had faced the challenges and conquered their fears, insecurities and rejection and awakened to a new hope and a new future.

He had not caused this path to unfold – that occurred simply through the greediness and selfishness of man, but he had used the obstacles to help them find themselves again. They were a delight to him.

He wandered over to the golden book, thumbing the thick pages open. He looked at the empty pages that lay ahead for their lives. They would write their own story - a story full of hope, joy and love - a story that would change the world.

⌘

## The Reckoning

### Book 2 of the Destiny Chronicles

Four years have passed since the Hamilton family escaped the clutches of the Dark Lord to make a new life for themselves. Aislinn Hamilton embarks on a new journey to follow her dreams and to change the world. Her idealistic world is turned upside down when she meets a man who stirs her heart and infuriates her at the same time. He will lead her back to the past she has tried so hard to forget – a past she does not wish to repeat.

Aislinn will discover shocking truths about herself, the man she thinks she loves, and the Great One himself.

The Reckoning is a story of love and truth and the need to fight for them. The real question is, can one ever truly escape one's past or is there always a reckoning that follows when secrets are revealed?

Book 2 of the Destiny Chronicles is to be published in 2015

# ABOUT THE AUTHOR

Caroline Hemingway lives in Melbourne Australia with her husband Hamilton and their four children. The Destiny Chronicles were birthed when she undertook putting pen to paper as a therapeutic exercise, discovering in the process a love of writing. This was followed by short stories and children's books she hopes yet to publish. She and her family are Foster carers to children who are at risk in the community and she is passionate about human rights. She is also an enthusiastic blogger and loves all things creative.